Crazy

Stupid

Obsession

A *Crazy Love* Novel

MELISSA TOPPEN

Crazy Stupid Obsession

Written by Melissa Toppen

TABLE OF CONTENTS

*Love isn't perfect. It's crazy. It's stupid.
It's messy. It's flawed.
That's what makes it so damn beautiful.*

Chapter One

Gavin

Fucking Decklan... He's my brother. Not by blood but that doesn't matter. I'd take a bullet for him and him for me. But right now I'm thinking I'd be more likely to fucking kill him myself than rather die for him.

Of course, none of this is his fault.

I'm the one who chose to pull Kimber into this which is what ultimately put me in this little predicament. I knew I needed Kimber. Decklan needed her. I didn't know what else to do. He's been sitting at Conner's grave for damn near four hours, and she's the only one that can seem to talk any sense into his stupid ass. Though I never thought I'd see the day when a woman would have that much power over him.

Regardless, I should have insisted Harlee not come with us. But even I know no matter how hard I tried to prevent that from happening, she would have ended up coming just the same. Kimber's her friend, her roommate, and if there's one thing I've learned about Harlee Travers it's that she's fiercely loyal and protective of the people she cares about.

I wish I could say her mistrust in me is misplaced, but even I know that's not the case. She sees me, maybe clearer than anyone else does. The thought is more than a little unnerving.

I try to block out the hushed conversation taking place next to me and focus my attention outside, but it doesn't do me much good. Hearing her giggle into the phone to *Bryan*, the guy she's apparently dating, is enough to make my blood boil, though I'm not entirely sure why.

"I know. I'm sorry. I promise I'll make it up to you." I watch her out of the corner of my eye as she talks.

I don't know why it bothers me so fucking much, but right now the urge to grab the phone from her hand and tell this Bryan fuck that she's mine is damn near overwhelming.

Mine? I don't even understand the

notion.

We fucked... Once.

Yeah it was good, and yes I have thought about it more than I probably would a normal hook up, but that doesn't mean I suddenly have some claim on her, or that I even want one for that matter.

"So, how long have you two been seeing each other?" I ask the question the moment she disconnects the call and lowers the phone from her ear, trying my best to sound as casual and unaffected as possible.

"Not long." She pushes her long blonde hair over her shoulder and turns her gaze out the window, staring out into the darkness.

I can see her face in the reflection of the glass, the dash lights illuminating her in the softest glow. I find myself momentarily distracted by how fucking beautiful she is.

I shake my head, trying to pull myself out of my haze.

I'm fucked up over all the shit Deck is going through and making sure his crazy ass is taken care of. I must just be off my game.

I need to get fucking laid, for starters.

"Is it serious?" Another question falls from my mouth like vomit I can't seem to swallow down.

Is it serious?

Am I fucking serious right now with these stupid ass fucking questions?

"What, are we friends now?" She snaps her head toward me, narrowing her gaze.

"Just trying to make conversation." I give her an innocent smile to which she reacts with an eye roll before turning back toward the window.

I reach out and rest my hands on top of the steering wheel, letting out a loud breath. There's something about sitting this close to Harlee that has me all sorts of fucked up. It doesn't help matters that she seems to have an issue with me, though it's not hard to guess why.

I really wish she hadn't come. I have no idea how long we will be sitting here. Every minute that ticks by becomes that much more difficult not to pull her into my lap and feel her tight and wet around me.

Fuck.

Why did I tell Deck I would steer clear of her again?

I mean, not that he ever asked me to stay away from her. That's not his style. But out of respect for him and Kimber, I thought it best that I not add insult to injury where Harlee is concerned.

I'm fully aware of my ability to royally fuck everything up. I don't want to make things more difficult for Decklan. He's going through enough shit right now as it is.

Even still, I bet Harlee would happily let

me fuck her again if I made the first move. Her anger is a smoke screen, a useless tactic to try to throw me off her real issue. She's not mad that I didn't come running to her after we fucked. She's mad because she wants to fuck me again despite the fact that I completely blew her off.

Fuck. I'm a little mad, too.

A small laugh escapes my lips at the thought, causing Harlee to shift in her seat. I flip my eyes to the side, my gaze instantly falling to the inside of her thigh where her black dress has ridden up slightly. I immediately feel myself start to tighten at the thought of running my hands along her smooth flesh.

Fuck... I really *do* need to get laid.

"I wonder what's going on out there." When she finally speaks she doesn't look in my direction. Instead, she continues to peer into the darkness, clearly just trying to fill the silence that has now settled around us.

"Who knows?" I shrug.

"So what's his deal anyway?" She finally meets my gaze, the green specks in her hazel eyes standing out in the dim lighting.

"Who Decklan?" I question.

"No, Prince Charles," she bites sarcastically as she rolls her eyes. "Yes Decklan," she tacks on.

"Not my shit to tell." I shrug.

"I'm not asking for his life story." She doesn't seem the least bit offended by my lack of an answer. "I just want to know what he's like, considering he's dating my roommate who happens to be a very good friend of mine."

"Why don't you ask Kimber?" I bounce my leg, growing increasingly more impatient.

"Because she loves him," she answers simply.

"What the fuck does that have to do with anything?" I arch my brow curiously.

"Love is blind, or have you never heard that before?" She studies me for a long moment.

"That's just what people say so they have an excuse to overlook other people's stupid shit," I snap, deciding if I don't get out of this truck right fucking now I'm gonna crawl out of my skin.

Pushing the driver's side door open, I slide out, slamming it behind me. At first, I think Harlee is going to stay where she is, but seconds later I hear the passenger door creak open followed by the sound of her heeled feet as they hit the pavement.

"I take it you've never been in love before?" She rounds the truck, continuing our conversation without skipping a beat.

When I throw her an annoyed glare she changes tactics.

"All I'm saying is that Kimber is too in love with Decklan to see his flaws. As his best friend, I assume you know him better than anyone else. I just want to know if he's a good guy."

"Because I would tell you if he wasn't?" I shake my head, reaching into my jacket pocket to pull out my pack of cigarettes.

Sliding one out, I hold it between my lips as I search my pockets for a lighter.

"Here." Harlee's voice causes me to look up.

She has her hand extended, a small pink lighter clenched between her perfectly manicured fingertips.

"Thanks," I grumble, taking it from her.

"You know you really shouldn't smoke those," she tacks on after I've lit the cigarette and taken one long, hard drag.

"Let me guess, because they give you cancer." I pin my eyes on hers and take another deep inhale.

"Among other things." She takes her lighter back and slides it into the small purse clutched in her hand.

"My friend Paxton's mom just passed away from lung cancer and she never smoked a day in her life. Everything will kill you. Might as well go out my way." I shrug, taking another drag from the cigarette. "Why the hell do you even have a lighter, since you clearly don't smoke?" I tack on.

"Never know when you might need it."
She crosses her arms in front of her chest and
leans back against the side of the truck.

I think on her statement for a moment
before finally deciding to answer her original
question.

"He's a good guy."

"Huh?" She turns her face toward me,
clearly not able to keep up with the quick
change in conversation.

"Decklan. You asked if he was a good
guy. He is. Probably one of the most loyal
fuckers to ever walk the face of the earth. And
he loves Kimber. Never thought I'd see the day
that would happen but there it is. Good
enough for you?" I ask.

"Good enough for me." A slow smile
spreads across her face. "How long have you
two known each other?" she asks.

"What, are we friends now?" I repeat
her previous statement back to her, letting out
a slow exhale of smoke.

She glares at me for a long moment. I
can see the gears shifting inside that pretty
little head of hers before she even opens her
mouth to speak again.

"No, we're not." She breaks my gaze,
looking away for a long moment before finally
finding my eyes again. "Since you're not
worried about sparing my feelings, why don't

you tell me why you've avoided me like the plague since the night we hooked up?"

"I haven't avoided you." I take another hit of the cigarette before dropping it to the ground.

"No?" She cocks her head to the side, her forehead scrunching together. "Pretty sure I tried reaching out, even suggested we hang out again. You blew me off with some bullshit excuse about having to work the bar that night."

"I work the bar most nights." I struggle to see what she's getting at.

"But my roommate is dating the other owner of the bar. Did you think I wouldn't know if you actually worked the bar that night or not?" She's trying to keep her face void of emotion but it's clear this bothers her more than she's likely to admit. "I guess I should have known better huh?" She hugs her arms tighter around herself when a cool breeze whips around us.

The wind catches her long blonde hair causing it to dance freely in the air. It's one of those moments that would make an incredible photograph. She's definitely more beautiful than any model I've ever seen. Her tall, slender body tucked up against my large truck. Her hair flying wildly around her beautiful face. Her hazel eyes cutting through the night like razors.

She really is fucking breathtaking.

"What's that supposed to mean?" I finally blurt, not sure that I really want to know the answer to the question.

"I know what kind of man you are, Gavin. I knew the night I slept with you. And yet I did it anyway." She shakes her head, clearly regretting that decision.

Her reaction doesn't sit well with me. I don't want to be someone she regrets and yet, without even meaning to, that's exactly what I am.

"What kind of man is that exactly?" My voice comes out a bit harsher than I intend for it to.

"The kind of man who fucks any woman he wants with no regard for her feelings." She meets my gaze straight on.

"I made no promises to you and yet you were still more than eager to climb up on my cock. I'm pretty fucking sure I gave you exactly what *you* wanted." I take a couple of steps toward her, closing the distance between us until she is caged between me and the truck.

She's so close I can smell the traces of the vanilla body wash that lingers on her perfect fucking skin. Her full, pink lips are just inches from mine. Now centimeters.

I stop just shy of her mouth, smiling when her breath catches and her entire body tenses.

"That's what I thought," I breathe against her lips.

I fight the urge to taste her and take a step back, watching the disappointment flash across her face before it's immediately replaced by anger.

"Fuck you, Gavin," she spits before whipping around and heading back toward the passenger door.

"Pretty sure you already did." I can't stop myself from saying it.

She hits me with a look of disbelief and then climbs into the truck, slamming the door shut behind her. I immediately regret my statement but can't bring myself to apologize for making it.

It's better this way; her hating me. At least if she hates me, then she takes away my power to hurt her. Because if given the opportunity I have no doubt that I would fucking destroy her and that tough little exterior she hides behind.

Chapter Two

One month later...

<u>Harlee</u>

"Please tell me you're free New Year's Eve," Kimber says seconds after pushing her way inside our dorm room, her cheeks red from the cold outside.

"Hello to you, too," I laugh, looking up from my Kindle to watch her enter.

It's been three days since she's made an appearance, and by the looks of her, I'd say she's had very little sleep over the course of that time. Compliments of Decklan I'm sure.

"Seriously. I just found out *Deviants* is throwing a huge New Year's Eve party. You can't make me go alone," she whines, flopping down on her bed.

"Will Decklan be there?" I ask, considering he's one of the co-owners of *Deviants*.

"Of course," she sighs, kicking off her shoes before pulling a hair band off her wrist. She ties her long, blonde waves into a messy bun on top of her head before pinning her blue eyes back on me.

"Well, then you won't be alone." I roll my eyes, turning my attention back to the book I'm reading.

"Yes, I will be." I read two words before she interrupts me. "Even if he *takes the night off*." She puts air quotes around the phrase. "It's still his place of business and you know he's going to be busy handling fifty different things which will leave me sitting at the bar all by myself wishing I had an amazingly awesome, beautiful, wonderful friend there with me." She puckers out her bottom lip at me.

"No." I shake my head, not even willing to consider it.

"Really?" she huffs, clearly surprised by my immediate and exact answer.

"Really." I lock my Kindle and toss it to the end of the bed. "I have successfully erased all traces of Gavin Porter from my life, and now you want me to willingly walk back into the lion's den? Absolutely not." I shake my head, feeling my face turn up in disgust.

It's one thing to know that Gavin exists; it's another to acknowledge said existence which is exactly what I have refused to do these past few weeks.

"You slept with him once," Kimber protests. "I get that it didn't turn out the way you wanted, but are you seriously going to continue to let that man have that much power over you?" she questions. "The Harlee I know never lets a man dictate her life."

I know what she's trying to pull, but it won't work. I wish I could say that it's just my pride holding me back but that's not entirely the truth. I'm scared to see him again. The last time we saw each other was over a month ago and the tension between us was so thick I felt like I could barely breathe.

"I just have no desire to surround myself with *those* kinds of people." I throw my legs over the side of the bed and turn to face Kimber head on.

"Those kind of people?" She hits me with an offended look.

"I didn't mean you and Decklan." I immediately move to explain, "I just think it's best that I remove myself from any situation that involves people like Gavin."

"You're so busy trying to hate him that you can't even see the real problem can you?" she questions, cocking her head to the side.

"What are you talking about?" I bite,

annoyance clear in my voice.

"You're just like him. You are the female version of Gavin." Her tone is absolute. "You can't stand that for the first time ever, a guy didn't want more than a hookup from you. Normally you hold the power to make those decisions. You get to decide if you want to date the guy or leave it as a one-time thing, but with Gavin, you don't get to do that. He's taken your power away and you can't stand it."

"That's not true," I insist, feeling the familiar twist in my stomach.

If I'm being honest with myself, Kimber has a point. But I'm not about to admit that to her.

"And," she tacks on, pulling my attention back to her, "I think you still really like him."

"Yeah right," I object, shaking my head adamantly.

"Then prove it," she challenges. "Come with me. You can bring Bryan. What better way to show Gavin you don't care?" She says in a way that has more meaning behind it than she lets on. "Besides, you know Angel will be down if you are."

Of course, I know she's right. My crazy, fearless, best friend, Angel, is always down for a good time. She would probably jump at the chance to spend New Year's in Portland.

"I don't know," I murmur.

"Please?" she draws out. "Angel can bring that new boy toy of hers, too. What's his name again?" She giggles at her inability to recall his name.

"Trenton," I laugh.

"God I still can't wrap my mind around the fact that someone actually reeled that girl in." She shakes her head in disbelief.

"It's only been like five minutes. Let's not get ahead of ourselves," I remind her. "Angel has dated several men over the course of our friendship and not one has managed to hang onto her for more than a month. She's too much of a free bird to be held down by the confines of a relationship."

"I don't know. She's all glassy eyed where this one is concerned," Kimber interjects. "So what do you say?" She jumps back to the matter at hand. "*Deviants*? New Year's Eve?" She puckers her bottom lip out even further than before.

"Let me talk to Bryan." I finally concede, knowing she's not going to give up on this easily.

She lets out a little squeal and jumps from the bed, bouncing toward me. Only seconds pass before her arms are around my neck and she's squeezing me tightly.

"Thank you. Thank you. We are going to have a blast. You'll see." She releases me, turning to grab my phone from the bedside table. "Now call that man of yours and tell him the plan." She tosses the device in my lap.

"You're awfully bossy, you know that?" I laugh. "What happened to my sweet, quiet Kimber? I kind of miss that Kimber," I joke.

"No one misses that Kimber." She scrunches her nose. "That Kimber was lame. Now call." She points to my phone. "I'll text Angel and let her know. This is going to be so much fun!"

"Yeah, so much fun," I mumble under my breath as I pull up Bryan's number and hit call.

Kimber disappears into the bathroom before the second ring sounds in my ear.

Leaning back, I rest my head against the large stack of pillows piled at the head of my bed and gaze up at the ceiling, momentarily distracted by my thoughts of Gavin. When Bryan's voice finally comes across the line, he has to say hello twice before I even realize he's answered.

"Hey," I chime in.

"Hey." There's a smile in his voice and it immediately brings a smile to my face.

I like Bryan, a lot. It wasn't instant, and he certainly doesn't give me the intense rush that I get when I'm around Gavin, but there is a slow simmer there. They say some of the strongest feelings are those that build slowly over time so that's what I'm giving it— time.

"So how do you feel about spending New Year's in Portland?" I ask, twirling a piece of hair around my finger as I speak.

"Will you be there?" Again, I can hear the smile in his voice.

"Um, well yeah," I laugh lightly into the phone.

"Then I'm there." His answer is instant.

"Don't you want to know where we're going?" I object.

"As long as I'm with you, I don't care where we are."

"Is that so?" I can't fight the smile on my lips.

This is how it should be: easy, uncomplicated. He wants me, it's that simple. I'm determined not to take that for granted.

"It is." His voice drops lower. "What are you doing right now?"

"Laying in bed," I answer as seductively as I can muster, trying to make my situation sound much sexier than it actually is.

"Are you now?" There's laughter in his voice.

I open my mouth to respond but before I can get anything out a loud knock sounds against the door. I jump slightly, startled by the sudden noise.

"Crap. Hang on." I push myself out of the bed and quickly cross the room.

Peeling open the door, I am immediately

greeted by shaggy blond hair and chocolate brown eyes. Bryan.

I keep the phone to my ear. "Hey, I gotta go. Some really hot guy just showed up at my door and looks as though he's in need of entertaining." I smile widely.

"Oh, well, by all means, don't keep the poor lad waiting." He disconnects the phone, his arm snaking around my waist moments later. "Hey," he breathes against my mouth before pressing a gentle kiss to my lips.

"What are you doing here?" I ask, pulling back slightly.

"I was on my way up when you called. I missed you," he admits, kissing me again. "Is Kimber here?" He looks inside the room, hitting me with mischievous eyes the moment he sees the room is empty.

"Bathroom." I gesture toward the closed door along the far wall.

"Rats. Foiled again," he laughs, rubbing the tip of his nose against mine before his lips find mine again.

This time, the kiss isn't so innocent and he tightens his grip on my body, making sure I feel the hardness of him against my stomach. By the time he pulls back, I'm a bit out of breath and wishing Kimber wasn't here so he could do exactly what he came here to do.

"Come in." I pull out of his arms and drag him into the room, closing the door behind him.

"So Portland huh?" He crosses the room, flopping down on the end of my bed.

"Yeah. Kimber's boyfriend, Decklan, owns a bar there," I start.

"I've heard you mention it," He interjects.

"Apparently, they're having a huge party and she really wants us to go. Decklan will probably be busy and she doesn't want to end up sitting at the bar alone."

"I get that." He gives me a sweet smile, and my heart melts a little.

He really is the nicest guy. Born and raised on the coast of California, he is the definition of a West Coast surfer. With shaggy blond hair, tan skin, and a lean muscular body, it's clear he's spent many years on the water. He's also very laid back and easy going. There's hardly a thing that seems to bother him. At least not from what I have seen in the few weeks we've been seeing each other.

"So you're sure you're okay with going?" I ask, stepping in between his legs and wrapping my hands around the back of his neck.

He peers up at me with a dimple-filled smile and nods.

"You really are something else, you know that?" I lean forward and kiss the top of his head before resting my cheek against it.

His arms close around my waist, and he holds me there for several long moments. It's times like this that I wish I could make myself feel something more intensely for Bryan. He's everything I should want and yet, there's something I want more.

I want to feel challenged. I want to feel passion. I want to feel fire consume me when he touches me instead of just the warmth of his skin against mine. For a brief moment, Gavin's dark blue eyes flash through my mind, and my heart rate immediately accelerates.

Suddenly guilt floods through me. As much as I say I don't want to see Gavin, and as much as I try to convince myself that I'm going to *Deviants* for Kimber, deep down I know that's simply not the whole truth.

I also know that in some small way I'm hoping that showing up there with Bryan will make Gavin jealous. I know it's wrong and a completely ridiculous thought, but it's exactly the direction my mind is going in until Kimber appears from the bathroom and snaps me from my haze.

"Bryan." She smiles, tightening the towel wrapped around her head.

"Nice to see you, Kimber." He pulls back from our embrace and gives her a warm smile. "How are you enjoying your winter break so far?"

"I'm kind of going crazy," she admits on

a laugh. "The restaurant has been pretty slow since so many students have gone home for break so I haven't gotten many shifts. Without class to fill my time, I kind of feel rather lost."

"I know what you mean. This is the first break I haven't spent in California. Kind of feels like a ghost town." His words pull my attention back to him.

I narrow my gaze on him as I slide down next to him on the bed.

"I thought you always just went home on Christmas Eve and day?" I ask, confused.

"You assumed." He takes my hand and squeezes.

"Then why didn't you spend your break at home this year?" I question.

Bryan is a junior, whereas Kimber and I are only freshman, so this is the third winter semester he's been through.

"I thought that was pretty obvious." He gives me a warm smile and the guilt I was feeling just moments ago intensifies tenfold.

"Was your family disappointed not to have you home for the month?" Kimber chimes in, flipping her head over to rub the excess water out of her hair with the towel.

"They were okay with it. I have four siblings so my parents have plenty of family around."

"That must be nice." Kimber straightens, dropping the towel into the laundry basket next to her bed. "Having so many siblings," she adds, grabbing a hairbrush from her nightstand.

"It's okay... Sometimes," he laughs. "Three of them are teenage girls so even if I was at home, I'd likely not be at *home*."

"I think I can understand that." Kimber lets out a small giggle and then pauses, immediately changing directions. "So do you two have plans today?" she asks, ripping the brush through her thick hair in an attempt to rid it of its tangles.

"No, I just stopped by to see my girl." Bryan nudges my shoulder with his and gives me a warm smile.

"You two are too cute." Kimber smiles warmly at us, her blue eyes firmly fixed on my face.

"What are you up to?" I ask her.

"Well..." She hesitates, looking to Bryan and then back to me. "I was hoping I could steal you for a while. Maybe go grab some dinner. Catch up."

"Well don't let me get in the way of your plans, ladies." Bryan immediately stands.

"Are you sure?" I object, feeling bad that he came here just to turn around and leave again.

"Of course," he reassures me. "I have a few things I need to take care of. Call me when you get back." He winks, leaning down to lay another light kiss to my mouth.

"Take care of my girl, Kimber." He nods in her direction.

"Always do." Her smile widens as she watches him cross the room and disappear into the hallway moments later.

"Oh my god. He totally worships you," she whisper screams, doing a weird little victory dance in the middle of the room.

"He does, doesn't he?" I let out a slow exhale.

"Why do I get the feeling that isn't a good thing?" Kimber immediately falls serious, sliding down onto the edge of her bed to sit directly across from me.

"It is. It really is. He's amazing. It's just... I don't know. Something's missing," I admit, hoping she understands.

"What do you mean?"

"I don't know. How do you feel when you're with Decklan?" I ask, hoping to explain it another way.

"Amazing. Electrified. Alive," she rambles off.

"Exactly. That's how it should feel. At least I feel like that's how it should feel."

"And you don't feel that way?" She gestures to the door where Bryan just exited.

"I like him," I admit. "It's just mild and comfortable. There's no real spark."

"Give it some more time. Maybe it'll

come." She hits me with a reassuring smile.

"Yeah, maybe." I shrug. "So where are you wanting to go?" I ask, desperately wanting to get away from this topic of conversation and focus on something else.

"Madrins?" Kimber smiles, knowing there is no way I will ever say no to their incredible crab cakes.

"You're on." I push off of the bed and head for the bathroom. "Give me ten minutes," I call back over my shoulder.

"I'll give you five," she challenges, laughing when I stick my tongue out at her before playfully slamming the bathroom door behind me.

Chapter Three

Gavin

"Well if it isn't my pussy-whipped best friend. He's alive." I torment Decklan the moment he emerges from his apartment above the bar.

His wrinkled white shirt and faded jeans are a clear indication to how little of a fuck he gives about his appearance at the moment. If I had to guess, I'd say this is the first time he's been out of bed in the last two days.

"What the fuck are you doing here already?" He arches a brow when he sees the beer sitting on the bar in front of me. "Little early isn't it?"

"Since when do you give a fuck how

early it is?" I bite, watching a slow smile spread across his face.

"Good fucking point," he agrees, sliding behind the bar to retrieve a beer for himself.

He pops the top off the bottle and takes a long swig before crossing around the counter and sliding into the bar stool next to me.

"Kimber gone?" I ask, lifting the bottle to my lips.

"Yeah, she took off yesterday afternoon. She had a few things to take care of. She'll be back soon." He runs a hand through his messy dark blond hair.

"You ever gonna cut that shit?" I gesture to where a large chunk of hair is now hanging directly in front of his eye.

"No," he answers dryly, pushing the hair aside.

"We need to make a decision about Paxton." I slide the beer bottle back and forth between my hands, the glass making a scratching noise across the surface of the bar.

Paxton is an old friend of mine and Decklan's. His mom shipped him to Oregon to live with his dad after he got himself in a bit of a mess in California. He couldn't have been but thirteen at the time. It's hard to wrap my head around the fact that these two fuckers have been around for literally half of my life.

"Yeah," Deck agrees, pulling me back to the conversation. "What nights does he want to play again?"

"I told him Sunday through Thursday would work, but I'm not sure he wants to play every night. I was thinking we would give him maybe Sunday and Wednesday and then he can pick up extra shifts as he wants. This place is dead as fuck Monday and Tuesday nights anyway. It doesn't make much sense for us to pay a live act."

Paxton is the musician of our group and one hell of one at that. Considering he's been crashing on my couch since he arrived back in Oregon a few weeks ago, I'm eager to give him something to do.

He's been living in California for the past several months, taking care of his mom who just recently passed from cancer. Given the size of his inheritance, I know money isn't the issue. It's more about being around people and having something to do.

"Might bring in more business, though," Decklan adds, taking a long drink of his beer, draining half the bottle in one gulp. "But yeah, Sunday and Wednesday works for me. Did you nail down the specifics for the New Year's party?"

"Yeah, I'm gonna have Paxton start off the night with an acoustic set and then *Technolights* will go on at ten and play til close," I say, referring to one of the hottest cover bands in the Portland area.

"Perfect," he says, turning toward the door the moment it swings open.

Sunlight filters into the dimly lit bar shrouding Kimber in a sea of yellow as she steps through the doorway. I remember the first time I laid eyes on this girl. Such an innocent, quiet thing. Beautiful of course, almost angelic in a way. But I have learned over the course of the past couple of months that she is so much more than the little good girl I had her pegged for.

For starters, she can handle Decklan. She's on a very short list in that department. Anyone that can handle my moody, asshole of a best friend deserves a medal. I've also got a hell of a lot of respect for her, especially after everything she's done for him. She's changing him in a way I never dreamed possible.

She's given him a spark and brought a bit of life back to him that I haven't seen since before his brother Conner died in a car accident a few years back.

The moment the door closes behind her on a loud thud, her eyes immediately bounce between me and Decklan and then to the beers on the counter.

"Really, guys?" She shakes her head, making her way toward us.

"Decklan did it." I point jokingly at Deck who lets out a full belly laugh.

"What is she your mother?" He shakes

his head. "Decklan did it." He mimics my statement.

"Fuck you, dude." I shove at his shoulder, effectively pushing him out of the bar stool.

He slides onto his feet and flips me off seconds before dropping an arm around Kimber's shoulder and pulling her into him.

"You get everything taken care of?" he asks, kissing the side of her head.

I don't know why but the action makes my stomach turn a bit. It's clear to see how crazy they are about each other and while I couldn't be happier for Decklan, that doesn't mean I want to sit here and watch them give each other googly eyes.

"Yeah. I was able to work out picking up a couple extra shifts at the restaurant, thank god." She sighs.

"Getting tired of me already are you?" he teases.

"Shut up." She giggles, laying a light smack on his stomach. "If I want to be able to eat next semester, I need to work."

"Yeah because I would let you starve." He pins serious eyes on her.

"It's not your job to take care of me. I pay my own way, end of discussion."

"I'll show you end of discussion," he growls playfully.

"Oh and I also invited Harlee and Angel

to the party Thursday night." She ignores his comment, turning her gaze on me. "I hope that's okay," she adds. "I'm pretty sure Bryan and Angel's new... Well, I'm not sure what you would call him," she laughs, "are going to come, too." Her eyes study my face for a long moment before turning back up to Decklan.

"Fine by me." Decklan smiles down at her, tucking a blonde wave of hair behind her ear.

Not fucking fine by me I want to say, but I keep my mouth shut. I finish off the remainder of my beer in one swift drink.

"Is that okay with you, Gavin?" She settles her soft smile in my direction, lifting her eyebrows slightly in question.

"I don't give a fuck," I answer casually on a shrug, pushing out of the bar stool. I cross to the trash can and drop my empty beer bottle inside. "I'm gonna party and fuck my way into the new year no matter who is here."

"Okay then." Her smile widens.

I don't know why but I get the sinking feeling there is something behind that smile of hers. What's in my reaction that clearly has her amused?

I slide behind the bar, grabbing a few near empty bottles of liquor. Setting them on the back counter, I grab a pen and paper and start jotting down what we're getting low on so

I can make sure to get it ordered in time for Thursday.

Deviants is mine and Decklan's baby. We bought this bar a few years back. Sunk every penny we owned into fixing it up and turning it into the successful business it is now. We still handle the everyday operations, both of us too big on control to hire a manager to handle anything for us.

"Don't forget to order extra champagne." Decklan's voice sounds from behind me.

"Got it." I nod without turning. "Oh shit, I almost forgot." I spin toward them just as they are about to head upstairs. "Mom wanted me to invite you to dinner tomorrow night."

"What's the occasion?" Decklan asks, clearly not missing the fact that it's only been a week and a half since our *monthly* Tuesday night Spaghetti dinner. Which is a tradition in the Porter household and one Decklan has attended for years.

Hell, he's practically family. No, he is part of the family.

"Charlie's coming home," I say, referring to my younger sister who has been living with my aunt Pam in New York for the past three years while attending NYU.

"Seriously?" Decklan seems as surprised as I did when Mom told me the news. "Is she just visiting?" he adds.

"No, apparently she's home for the

foreseeable future."

"Really? I thought she had another year?" he questions.

"Charlie, as in your younger sister?" Kimber interrupts, clearly a little bit out of the loop.

"Yeah," I confirm. "She left after finishing high school." I don't mention that I have only seen her once the entire time she's been gone.

"How long has that been?" she asks.

I have to remind myself that Kimber is new to this whole family circle. Decklan, of course, already knows the details where Charlie is concerned.

"Three years now." I look to Deck for confirmation.

He nods in agreement before speaking again. "Shit. Has it really been that long?"

"She's twenty-one now," I say.

It seems crazy to think of her being that old.

Being four years younger than me, I've always been extremely protective of her, as has Deck. I think in a lot of ways she resented that about me and that's why she's made herself so scarce over the past couple of years. Of course, deep down, I think the main reason she hasn't been coming home to visit is because it's not the same here without Dad.

"Fuck." Decklan pulls me back to the

present. He runs another hand through his hair, shaking his head in disbelief. "Twenty-one."

"Hard to believe." I nod in agreement. "So you think you can make it?"

"Yeah man, you know you can count me in," he answers.

"What about you, Kimber? You wanna join us?" I ask, knowing my mom would love to see her again.

Kimber has a love of art that my father had. It makes my mom so happy to have someone to talk *Art* with again. I think it reminds her of when my dad was still alive.

"Are you sure that's okay?" she questions. "I don't want to intrude."

"Are you kidding? You're part of the family now." I gesture between her and Decklan.

"Whether you want to be or not," Decklan teases, tucking her into his side.

"Then yes, of course." Her smile spreads from ear to ear.

"Six thirty," I confirm, waiting until Deck gives me a nod before turning back to finish my inventory.

Him and Kimber disappear upstairs moments later causing the silence of the room to settle around me. My mind immediately whirls back to what Kimber said earlier about Harlee coming Thursday night.

My fists clench involuntarily at the thought of having to watch her and that douche bag of a boyfriend hang all over each other all night. Then again, why the fuck do I care? I shake my head, trying to rid myself of whatever the fuck is causing my mind to focus on Harlee.

I need a distraction...

Dropping the pad of paper onto the counter, I slide my cell phone from my back pocket and scroll through the contacts. I click on Jenny's number the moment I see it, letting out a loud exhale as I place the phone to my ear.

Decklan may have had a strict rule about fucking the same girl more than once, before Kimber of course, but I'm a firm believer that a good pussy is a good pussy, no matter how many times you fuck it.

Jenny is my favorite go to. She's a feisty ginger that likes it rough and will take it any way I want to give it to her. While the women willing to let me stick my cock in them are a dime a dozen, very few are as adventurous as Jenny and right now, that's exactly what I need.

The phone rings for a third time before her bubbly voice comes across the line.

"Well if it isn't Gavin Porter." I can hear the smile in her voice.

"Jenny."

"I haven't heard from you in weeks. I was starting to think you were tired of me," she jokes.

"You busy?" I waste no time with pleasantries.

"Not at all." Her voice drops low.

"I'll be there in fifteen."

"Come on up. The door's unlocked," she purrs.

She's clearly not the least bit disturbed that I'm calling her for sex at ten thirty in the morning. Just another reason why she's the number I chose to call and not any of the others that I have lined up.

I end the call without another word, grabbing my keys off the back counter. Crossing toward the front, I slide the lock into place and then head out back where my truck is parked.

I may not be able to shake Harlee Travers out of my fucking head, but I am damn sure I can fuck her out of it.

Chapter Four

<u>Gavin</u>

Sweat pours off my back as I pound relentlessly into Jenny from behind, taking her so forcefully that she can barely manage to keep her feet planted on the ground. I roll my hips, letting the pleasure crawling up my spine take hold.

I ignore the voice in the back of my head; the one telling me that no matter how hard I fuck this girl, I won't be able to shake the nagging feeling that has plagued the pit of my stomach for the last month. But that doesn't mean I'm not desperate to try. I increase my speed, my body now teetering on the verge of exhaustion.

Jenny gives me no indication that she can tell something is off. It's been less than ten minutes and already she is falling apart below me for the second time. Her orgasm causes her to clench down around me, making her already tight pussy feel even tighter. I dig my fingers into her hips and thrust harder, losing myself in the sound of our two bodies slamming together; in the cries of pleasure sounding from beneath me.

It's fucking exhilarating.

A low growl forms at the base of my throat as I feel the build finally start to creep its way up. Harder and harder I plunge until finally I feel myself explode, spilling my load into the too tight condom.

Two more thrusts and I collapse down onto Jenny's back, my breath coming in short spurts as I try to catch it.

"That was…" Jenny pants out. "That was…" She tries again. "Fuck me, Gavin." She sighs into the mattress, turning her head to the side.

Without a word, I push up. Pulling my softening erection from her, I slide off the condom and drop it into the trash can that sits next to her bedside table. Snagging my pants from the floor, I have both legs in and am sliding the material over my hips before she even makes an attempt to move.

"Where are you going?" She seems

disappointed.

"I got shit to do." It's not a lie but it's not the complete truth either.

Sure I've got shit to do but not for a few hours and even then I'm sure I could get out of it. Working the bar is not a requirement; I do it because I love it. I love the simplicity of it. It's probably my favorite part of owning the bar.

"You can't stay an hour longer?" She rolls to her back, her small, perky tits on full display. "I think I could persuade you." She gives me a wicked smile, her tongue darting across her bottom lip.

"Told ya, got shit to do." I finally locate my shirt tucked half way under the bed. Leaning down, I snatch it up, throwing it over my head in a matter of seconds.

"I'll call you later." I throw her a backward glance before quickly exiting the bedroom, not sticking around to hear what I'm sure she was about to say.

I'm downstairs and pushing my way outside before I even have my jacket all the way on, determined to get the fuck out of here as quickly as possible.

It's nothing Jenny did, of course, she was fucking incredible per usual. It's more of where my fucking head is at right now. What the fuck is wrong with me? I haven't been myself since my last exchange with Harlee that night at the cemetery. While I think of her less and less as the days pass, Kimber mentioning her this morning was like striking a match to the box, and suddenly everything came back to life.

I don't want to fucking picture her with another man, let alone have to witness it happen right in front of me. I *was* looking forward to the party Thursday night. Now I wish like hell I could find a way to get out of going altogether.

How does one go about getting out of a party they are hosting?

Climbing in my truck, I fire the engine to life and crank up the heat. Unfortunately, only cold air billows from the vents because the vehicle hasn't had a chance to heat up. It's fucking freezing outside today despite the sun shining brightly overhead.

Dropping my head to the cold leather of the steering wheel, I let out a frustrated growl. What the fuck is it about this girl that has me so fucking obsessed with her?

Sure she's beautiful, but she's not the only fucking pretty female in the world. So what is it exactly that has me so strung up and not able to shake her?

I guess there's only one way to find out...

I have to fuck her again. I have to look into those beautiful eyes and watch her come undone with my cock deep inside her. I have to know once and for all why she seems to have this fucking hold on me.

With that, my tension relaxes. The heaviness seems to float away and for the moment, I feel somewhat normal again. I can't believe it took me so long to come to this conclusion. Maybe that's the issue. She's the only woman I have ever denied myself.

I have only been trying to stay away from her to not make Decklan's life any more difficult, but given that he seems to be doing better than ever, I think it's safe to assume he couldn't care less what I do.

Besides, I can only take this so far before I lose my fucking shit. My nature is revolting against me. I am not built to deny myself what I want and as such, this is my punishment.

"Then go fuck her, you stupid fuck." I can hear exactly what Decklan would say if I went to him with this issue. He knows me better than anyone. He knows I am incapable of holding out forever. Honestly, I'm surprised I've lasted this long.

The fact that she has a boyfriend doesn't hinder my resolve in the least. She may be his right now, but come Thursday night it will be my cock buried inside of her.

****

"What the fuck?" The words fall from

my mouth as my baby sister Charlie walks into the foyer and hits me with a brilliant smile. "What the hell happened to you?" I can't believe how grown up she looks.

"Good to see you, too, ass." She smiles widely before throwing her arms around my neck. "God I've missed you." She squeezes me incredibly tight.

"I've missed you, too," I admit, smiling down at her the moment she releases her grip on me. "What the fuck are you doing home?" I ask, sliding out of my jacket before tossing it onto the armchair that sits just inside the living room.

"I just needed a break." She lets out a slow breath, tucking a strand of long dark hair behind her ear.

She looks like the Charlie I remember but then completely different at the same time. She seems so much older, more mature. There's an air of heaviness that seems to surround her. Something that I've never noticed before.

I open my mouth to question the clear change in her but before I can get a word out she squeals, her eyes darting somewhere behind me. I turn just in time to see her slender, short frame disappear into Decklan's embrace.

"Decklan Taylor, as I live and breathe." She releases him, stepping back to get a good look at him.

He smiles down at her with the type of love you would expect to see between a brother and a sister. No, they aren't blood, but they might as well be. Decklan is not just my brother, he is hers as well. I know how much she helped him after Conner's death. There's no doubt that the feeling between the two of them is mutual.

"Charlie, I'd like you to meet Kimber." Charlie's eyes dart to the beautiful blonde at Decklan's side.

"Mom told me you had a girlfriend. I didn't believe her." She says more to Kimber than to Decklan. "It's so nice to meet you." She pulls Kimber into a hug like she's known her for years.

"It's nice to meet you, too," Kimber gets out, clearly taken aback by my sister's affection.

Kimber has already met my other sister, Mia. Let's just say she's not quite so warm and fuzzy. More like a judgmental bitch if you ask me. It's apparent that Charlie is not at all what Kimber was expecting.

"What's up, man?" I nod in Deck's direction as Charlie turns back toward me.

"What's up?" He reaches out, knocking his fist against mine.

"Oh god, you guys are still doing that fist bump nonsense," Charlie chimes in, her dark eyes bouncing back and forth between the two of us.

"Why mess with a good thing?' I shrug.

"Good to see some things never change." She giggles. "Come on, Kimber." Charlie snags her hand and drags her away from Decklan. "I'm dying to hear all about how the two of you met."

Kimber throws Decklan a surprised and somewhat scared expression as she is toted away by my younger sister. He shakes his head on a laugh, throwing her a playful wink.

"Does she seem weird to you?" I ask Deck the moment they disappear around the corner.

"Like she's trying too hard?" Decklan speaks exactly where my mind is at.

"Yep. Something's not right with her."

"I mean, we've only seen her once in three years, Gav. Let's not get ahead of ourselves. Time changes people," Decklan interjects.

"Yeah, no shit." I throw him a sideways glance.

He's changed more than anyone over these past few months. I sure as shit never expected him to be the first one to settle down with just one woman and yet, here he is.

"Just give her some time to get re-acclimated," he adds, ignoring my statement. "It's gotta be weird being back here after all this time. Did she say why she left New York?"

"Nope. Of course, I only got here about three minutes before you, so we haven't really had the chance to talk."

"Well you know your sister, if she wants you to know, you'll know. If she doesn't, then you won't." He shakes his head on a laugh.

"What's with you tonight?" I give him a curious glance.

He seems almost giddy and Decklan doesn't get giddy. Hell, up until a couple months ago he barely even fucking smiled.

"Nothing." His smile fades as he tries to reign himself in.

"Fuck you, dude, you're a horrible liar."

"Who's a liar?" Paxton appears out of nowhere, stepping up next to Decklan to join in on the conversation.

"When the fuck did you get here?" I turn toward him.

"Just now," he answers without looking in my direction. "Now what are we talking about?"

"Decklan over here smiling like a giddy school girl?" I gesture to Deck who rolls his eyes and laughs.

Standing in the living room of the house I grew up in, I think this is the first time we have all been under this same roof together since before Dad passed. It seems weird, how much things have changed. And yet oddly enough it almost feels like nothing has changed all at the same time.

Decklan manages to change the conversation from him to Paxton without even skipping a beat. Before I know it we are doubled over laughing as Paxton retells the story of when my mom caught him whacking it in the bathroom one night.

"I couldn't fucking help it. I hadn't gotten off in like three days," he interjects through his laughter.

"So you thought it was a good idea to sneak into a bathroom at your best friend's house and beat it?" Decklan holds his stomach as another bout of laughter rolls through him.

"No doubt. Fuck, dude, did you ever think to lock the door?" I tack on.

"Fuck you, guys." Paxton shoves my shoulder.

"Please tell me you're not talking about what I think you are." My mom appears in the doorway, even smaller and more petite than Charlie, wiping her hands on the light blue apron draped around her neck.

"Hi, Rosie." Paxton's laughter dies off instantly as he gives my mom an apologetic smile.

"Boys." She shakes her head, her auburn hair tied back so tightly it doesn't move as she does. "Well come on you three. Dinner's gonna be cold by the time you lot get in there."

She gestures for us to head into the dining room.

Paxton drops a kiss on her forehead as he passes and then Decklan pulls her in for a hug before he too disappears down the hall.

"How are you, my boy?" Mom stops me before I can pass, pinning her blue eyes directly on my matching ones.

"I'm good, Mom." I give her a warm smile before kissing her cheek. "Besides the fact that I'm starving." I drop my arm over her shoulder and walk with her into the dining room.

Various conversations and laughter dance around us as we enter, and I take a moment to soak it all in. Having Charlie and Paxton both back home seems strange but incredible at the same time. It feels good having everyone back together again. It's been far too long since our family has really felt whole.

Chapter Five

<u>Harlee</u>

I have knots in the pit of my stomach as we approach the long line that has formed outside of *Deviants*. Residing in the heart of Portland, the establishment is almost always hopping but tonight it's off the charts. There has to be at least a hundred people or more waiting to get inside.

I can't help but wonder how long these people will wait before finally giving up and going elsewhere. Considering it's New Year's Eve, I would think they wouldn't want to spend their opening moments of the new year standing outside in the freezing cold.

"Well, this just sucks," Trenton, Angel's

date, chimes in from behind me. "We'll never get in."

"Relax." Angel nudges her shoulder against his. "We got connections." She winks before taking off toward the entrance, Trenton fast on her heels.

I watch as she saunters up to one of the bouncers, placing her hand on his shoulder as she leans in and speaks directly into his ear. A slow smile spreads across his round face and he nods. She's clearly telling him more than just our names. I can't help but shake my head on a laugh.

Fucking Angel. That girl can make any man eat out of the palm of her hand. Especially tonight. She looks incredible. Not that she doesn't always, but tonight she really looks killer. The normal blue highlights that streak her shoulder length dark hair have been traded in for purple ones. The color accents the deep shade of her dress perfectly giving the almost black material a plum appearance.

I'm actually pretty surprised she brought Trenton with her. Usually on nights like tonight she likes to play the field. I know this means she must actually *like* this guy. I wish I could say that doesn't surprise me, but it kind of does. I mean, he's an attractive enough guy. Short dark hair, kind of bulky, eyes so dark they are almost black. Of course, his southern drawl doesn't hurt matters. I swear every time he calls her darlin' I melt a little. I'm just surprised when any man can hold my crazy best friend's attention longer than five minutes.

"Come on." I entwine my hand in Bryan's and drag him toward Angel and Trenton.

By the time we reach the two bouncers manning the door, Angel has already managed to get us inside. Of course, I knew that wouldn't be an issue. Kimber said she had us on the very short list of spots reserved for friends.

"Wow." Bryan sighs next to me the moment we step inside.

Per usual, the boys have gone all out. The glass top bar that extends the entire left side of the room is lined with bright green and purple lights giving it a glowing effect. A large ball made to look like the one in Times Square, only on a much smaller scale, hangs over the center of the dance floor, casting shadows of light across the large crowd of people gathered there.

I recognize the man standing on the stage almost instantly. Paxton, I think. I've only met him once, but I know he's a friend of Decklan and Gavin's. He strums his guitar effortlessly as he sings out over the crowd, his voice so seductive and raspy that within seconds goose bumps erupt across my skin.

It should be illegal to be that attractive and that talented all at the same time. His brown hair is short and perfectly styled, his facial hair well-kept with just enough scruff to make him even sexier than he would be otherwise. His clearly toned body is clad in dark jeans and a tight fitted V-neck white shirt that puts every one of his rippling ab muscles on full display. And while normally I would be melting on the spot watching this man perform, it's another man entirely that captures my attention and immediately causes my heart to gallop inside my chest...

Gavin.

He's standing off to the side of the stage, two women draped on either side of him. He's swaying back and forth, laughing like he doesn't have a care in the world. I wish it didn't bother me to see him like this but honestly, it sends an anger through me that I have trouble wiping off my face before anyone notices it's there.

"We should find Kimber," Angel hollers over the noise, pulling my attention to where she is standing next to me.

"Okay," I agree, tightening my grip on Bryan's hand as I finally look in his direction.

He's wearing that sweet carefree smile, scoping the room out like it's the coolest thing he's ever seen. The sight instantly calms the rage I felt only moments ago. Bryan is such a laid back, fun loving person. His laughter and smile are so infectious it's almost impossible to feel anything but happiness in his presence.

I need to focus on that. My fun, attractive, beach bum of a date and not the sexy as sin, bad boy, bar owner that seems to evoke so many different emotions from me that just one look has me feeling like my head is going to explode.

"Harlee," I hear Kimber's voice wash over the noise from the crowd, and I look to my right just in time to see her push through a group of people before stepping up next to me. "I'm so glad you could make it." She gives me a brief hug before turning to Angel who pulls Kimber directly into her chest.

"Hey sexy," Angel purrs playfully. "You look HOT!" She trails her eyes down Kimber's petite frame just seconds after releasing her. "I dare say I've rubbed off on you." She gestures to the red lace dress that makes Kimber look like she just stepped out of a fashion magazine. The material clings to her small frame, accenting her chest and hips before coming to a stop just inches above her knee. The fact that she has no idea how pretty she is makes her even more so.

"Oh God." Kimber fakes disgust. "Please say I don't look like, Angel." She turns toward me, a smile playing on her lips.

"Well." I shrug, laughing when her

mouth forms an O of surprise. "You don't look as slutty if that helps," I add playfully.

"It's nothing to be ashamed of," Angel tacks on, not the least bit offended by me and Kimber's obvious teasing. "Take pride in the fact that you can have any man in this entire room." She grins, ignoring the look of confusion that has taken over Trenton's face. "Don't worry. I've got my man," She reassures him, pushing up on her tiptoes to kiss his jaw.

"Yeah, so do I." Kimber smiles over my shoulder, her attention drawn to something approaching behind me.

I know it's Decklan before he even reaches us. I can tell by the way Kimber's skin flushes pink and her eyes take on an almost fogged expression. When he steps up next to her and pulls her into his arms, I try to ignore the ping of jealousy that coils in my stomach.

I'm not jealous because I want Decklan. Though he, like his friends, is impossibly attractive, he's always been Kimber's. That's what makes me jealous. The love, the passion, and the claim they seem to have on each other. It's like no one else exists when they're together. It's something I never really knew I wanted until I saw it up close.

They are such the perfect contradiction. Kimber's short and slender, reserved and proper. Always the good girl. Decklan is a tall drink of muscles and sexy hair. He's the drinker and the smoker. The ultimate bad boy. She's soft where he's hard. She's sweet where he's bitter. They make no sense and yet, they are perfect together.

"So glad you guys could make it." He finally turns his attention to our little group, his intense gray eyes bouncing between the four of us. "You must be Bryan." He extends his hand to the man standing next to me, using his other hand to push his hair out of his face.

"It's nice to meet you." Bryan takes his hand and gives it a brief shake.

"Trenton." Angel's date introduces himself next.

"Kimber has bracelets for everyone. You're on my tab for the night so enjoy yourselves." He gives us one last glance before leaning down and whispering something in Kimber's ear. She nods and gives him a sweet smile before he disappears back into the crowd.

"Come on," Kimber announces, cocking her head toward the bar before, setting off in that direction.

Moments later we are all supplied with bracelets that allow us to drink for the night. Despite the fact that Angel, Kimber, and myself are all under the age of twenty-one, Decklan has always allowed us to drink here which is definitely a perk because right now I could really use a shot. I feel so high strung and nervous. I wish I could say I didn't know why, but I know the exact cause for my feelings.

Kimber disappears a few minutes after showing us to a table she reserved for us along the far back wall. It's the perfect spot. It's far enough away from the dance floor that we can hear ourselves think but still in the heart of it all at the same time.

By the time the headlining act *Technolights* hits the stage several minutes later, I've managed to suck down two martinis. As soon as the catchy upbeat music thumps through the speakers, the four of us waste no time hitting the dance floor.

I spend the next hour and a half taking shots and dancing like a lunatic with Bryan who is even more fun with a couple of drinks in him. He slides across the dance floor like he owns the place, his moves putting everyone else's to shame.

When I excuse myself to run to the ladies room just ten minutes before midnight, I've almost forgotten all about Gavin Porter...

Almost.

It takes me several moments to push my way through the crowd as I make my way toward the back hallway that houses the bathrooms, my steps faltering the moment I see the line coming out of the small two-stall room.

Knowing there's no way I will be able to hold it that long, I cut back toward the bar where Kimber and Decklan are helping the three bartenders behind the counter pour and distribute glasses of champagne to the entire room to toast the new year.

"I need to use the bathroom." I mouth to Kimber who catches sight of me the moment I step up next to the bar.

Her eyes flick behind me to the bathroom line that is visible from where she's standing and then back to me. She nods, nudging Decklan in the ribs to get his attention. She turns toward him, no doubt asking him if I can use the restroom in his upstairs apartment. He too looks behind me at the line and then nods.

Seconds later Kimber grabs a set of keys from a hook next to the register and crosses toward me.

"Just make sure you lock it when you come down," she yells over the music, dropping the keys into my hand before spinning back toward the bar.

Knowing there isn't much time before the countdown, I quickly push my way inside the stairwell, locking the door behind me before climbing the stairs that lead up to Decklan's apartment two at a time.

I don't take any time to look around as I

quickly push my way inside and cross to the far wall where I know the bathroom is. Disappearing inside, I empty my bladder and wash my hands as quick as my extremely buzzed state will allow.

It isn't until I exit the bathroom moments later that I realize I'm not alone. I jump and scream when a voice washes over me, the sound instantly startling me.

"Having fun?" I recognize Gavin's deep voice the moment he speaks, even though his body is hidden in the shadows.

"Why are you up here and not downstairs enjoying *your* party?" I try to keep my tone even as I stare back at the silhouette of him on the couch.

"Why are you?" I can see the bottle as he lifts it to his lips but can't make out what exactly he's drinking.

The only light in the apartment is being provided by a street lamp that sits just a few feet from one of the windows along the back wall of the living room-bedroom combo. It offers enough light that we aren't blanketed in darkness but is still not enough to offer any real visibility into the small space.

I expect him to say something else, but he remains silent for several beats before finally pushing to his feet. He steps directly into the light filtering into the room, his blue eyes immediately locking on mine.

"I had to use the restroom," I stutter out, answering his previous question in an attempt to mask the sound of my heart beating against my ribcage.

"I gathered that much." His voice is laced with a hint of humor.

"Well, I should get back downstairs," I say, turning toward the door.

I get all of three steps in before Gavin's broad frame steps directly in front of me, effectively blocking my ability to exit.

"Or you could stay." He leans in so close I can feel his breath against my face.

"I don't think my *boyfriend* would like that very much," I bite, finally meeting his intense gaze.

"Boyfriend." It's not a question, it's a statement. One that he ponders for a long moment before a wide smile spreads across his impossibly handsome face.

My breath catches in my throat as he takes a commanding step toward me and then another. His steps forward match my steps backward until my back becomes flush with a wall and I can move no further.

"You got the boy part right." He runs his nose up my neck, inhaling deeply as he does.

A soft moan escapes my throat in spite of myself. No matter how much I want to hold it together, I can't seem to muster the strength to do so. My head is swimming with alcohol and the effects of the man pinning me between the wall and his hard muscular body.

"Mmm." He lets out a light chuckle at my reaction.

"He's more of a man than you are," I finally manage to choke out.

"Is that so?" His lips hover just inches from mine. "Tell me. Does your skin tingle under his touch like it does mine?" He trails the back of his hand down my arm, causing my skin to prickle beneath his touch.

"Does your body come to life for him like it does for me?" He trails his lips down my jaw causing heat to warm my body. "Does just the sound of his voice make you wet?" He slides his hand up the short length of my dress, his fingers grazing the now soaked material of my thong.

"Stop." The word is breathy and barely breaks the surface.

"You want me to stop?" he teases.

To my relief and disappointment, his hand immediately falls away, reappearing moments later when it clamps down on my hip.

"When you're ready for a real man, you know where to find me." The last word is barely off his tongue before his mouth crashes down on mine.

His kiss is hard and punishing. He's claiming me. He's making sure that I feel the effects of this kiss long after his lips leave mine. And I'm powerless to stop it. I melt into him, having no choice but to let him do with me what he will.

When he finally pulls back, I'm a disheveled mess of flushed skin and panting breaths. I hate that he has such an effect on me, and I hate even more that I let him see that effect.

"Happy New Year, Harlee," he breathes against my mouth before pushing away from me.

He spins, disappearing from the apartment before I can even muster the strength to speak. I stare at the back of the door for several long moments before Bryan's face flashes in front of my eyes.

Fuck.

I rush through the apartment and down the stairs, my weak legs protesting with each step I take. When I finally push my way into the bar, the entire crowd is humming with life. Champagne glasses are being lifted in toast and clanked together. Multicolored confetti floats through the air as couples embrace and friends hug.

I drop Decklan's keys onto the back of the bar and immediately start to scan the crowd trying to find Bryan, panic rising in my chest. What I find instead is Gavin, surrounded by at least four different women, all of which seem to be waiting to kiss him. I fight the shudder that runs through me when a tall, lengthy brunette steps up and shoves her tongue down his throat. His hand immediately skirts across her ass which is practically hanging out of the bottom of her too short skirt.

I swallow down the bile that rises in my throat, quickly spinning and setting off in the direction of our table. When I finally reach it, no one is there. I twist back around just in time to see Bryan making his way toward me, a wide smile across his cute face.

"Happy New Year." He pulls me into his chest the moment he reaches me.

"Happy New Year," I respond weakly, trying to act completely normal as he lowers his mouth to mine and lays a gentle kiss to my lips.

I try to ignore the lack of heat in that kiss. The lack of intensity or the passion that burns me from the inside out like Gavin's kiss does. I try to push all of that from my mind and try to focus on the man in front of me. The man who doesn't purposely toy with me or drape other women in my face. The sweet man who just wants to be with me.

"*Boy.*" Gavin's voice corrects me in my head.

Guilt washes through me when Bryan pulls back and hits me with another sweet smile. I'm forced to accept the reality of my actions and the repercussions those actions are likely to have. The last thing I want to do is hurt Bryan. I also don't want to lose him. Not for a man who has made it so very clear that this is just a game to him.

What a great way to start the new year. I let Gavin see that he has the upper hand with me. A position I never wanted to give away. I let him kiss me. I let him touch me. Hell, I wanted him to. And now I have to live with that choice.

Chapter Six

Harlee

"What's up with you?" My Aunt Joy asks, causing me to look up from the half-eaten sandwich on the plate in front of me.

Usually eating at my favorite deli always makes my day better, but today I am in no mood. Even my favorite Rueben on rye can't seem to shake the dark cloud hanging over me.

"What?" I question, trying to play if off like I have no idea what she's talking about.

"Harlee Rose Travers, I have known you for far too long to not know when something is up. And something is most certainly up. Spill." Her thin lips spread into a flat line as she gazes back at me.

Joy is the closest thing I have to a mother. Hell, she's really the only family I have left. The last piece of a family that was ripped apart by infidelity, theft, and drugs. My real mother was too busy popping pills and fucking random strangers to have any time to raise me. I had to learn to take care of myself at a very young age.

She died when I was ten. She left me alone with my criminal of a father that was no better of a parent than she had been. Of course, none of that mattered when he was sentenced to ten years in prison for armed robbery just two weeks after my fifteenth birthday.

I thought that was it. I thought for sure I was going to end up living on the streets or at best, in a group home. But then Joy came along. My father's only sibling, I didn't even know she existed until she showed up one day and told me that I was coming home with her.

Joy was six years younger than my dad. She had moved away at eighteen and married a wealthy man thirty years her senior. He died three years before she adopted me, leaving her with more money than she's likely to spend in her lifetime.

"Oh god, you're pregnant." She covers her mouth with her hand when I don't respond.

"I'm not pregnant." I shake my head adamantly.

"Oh thank god." Relief floods her face and for the first time, I notice the small wrinkles that line her eyes, intensifying her look of concern.

She's only in her mid-thirties and not a fan of aging. I learned that the hard way when I pointed out she had a gray hair once. She dropped everything and went directly to the salon. Over one gray hair!

She's rich and therefore all about appearances. If I point out the obvious signs that she's getting older, she will be on the phone scheduling Botox before anyone will be able to try and talk some sense into her.

"Cause you know I am way too young to be a grandma." She thinks on the statement. "Great aunt." She tosses it around. "Nope, either way, it just makes me sound old." She wrinkles her little nose in disgust, throwing her light brown hair behind her shoulders.

"Again, not pregnant." I don't try to hide my annoyance over this conversation.

"Then what is it?" She hits me with big hazel eyes; eyes that are almost an exact match to mine. "And don't say it's nothing. We both know you'd be lying."

"How did you know you loved Jack?" I ask, referring to her late husband.

She cocks a brow at me and studies me

curiously for a long moment before finally answering my question.

"I don't know. How does anyone know they love someone? I think you just know." She shrugs, swirling her manicured fingertip over the rim of her tea glass. "Why do you ask?" She bolts upright before I have a chance to respond. "Oh. My. God. Did you meet someone?" She looks at me like I have five heads.

"Why do you seem so surprised?"

"Really?" she blurts sarcastically, crossing her arms over her surgically-modified breasts as she leans back in the chair. "This from the girl who couldn't stand to go on a date with the same boy twice. I guess I just find it hard to believe that any guy would be special enough to tie you down."

"Two." My voice comes out strained.

"Two?" she questions, clearly not picking up what I'm trying to tell her.

"There are two of them." I bite my bottom lip. Just thinking about my situation makes my stomach want to reject everything I've managed to put in it in the last few minutes.

"Well don't just leave me sitting her in anticipation. Tell me everything." She leans forward, resting her elbows on the table in front of her.

She seems overly eager to hear what I

have to say. Like a paparazzi waiting for me to reveal some huge celebrity secret that's going to skyrocket their career instantaneously. Oddly enough, though, her reaction somewhat puts me at ease. It's hard enough talking to her about these things. I'm not the most open person. Hell, I've been seeing Bryan for weeks now and this is the first time I am even mentioning him to her.

Taking a deep breath, the words start flowing from my mouth. Once they do I can't make them stop. They pour from my lips one on top of the other, and before I know it, I have relived every last detail of the last three months out loud, including my last encounter with Gavin three days ago.

"What do you think I should do?" I finally let out a long sigh and relax back into my chair.

"I can't tell you what you should do, but it sounds to me like you already know," she says, taking a long drink of her iced tea.

"No, I don't. That's why I'm asking you," I object.

"It's clear who you want. I'm a firm believer in going with your gut. Had I listened to everyone when they warned me about marrying Jack, I would have missed out on the best ten years of my life. We didn't make sense and most of his family assumed I was marrying him for his money, but he knew better. He knew I loved him. God help me did I ever." Her eyes glass over as she speaks. "Every time that man stepped foot in the same room with me, my body would come to life. Even if I couldn't see him, I could always tell when he was near."

"Gavin." His name falls from my lips without even a thought. The moment it does I want to suck it back in and swallow it down.

I don't want it to be his name that falls from lips— his name makes my heart speed up— his name makes my skin burn. I don't want anything to do with him and yet, he's all I want. I know it without a second thought.

But that doesn't change the way I feel about Bryan, either. Over the last few weeks, I have come to really care for him. He makes me laugh. He holds me when I'm upset. Brings me flowers when I'm sad or stressed. He does everything he can to bring a smile to my face. Something has to be said about that too, right? It can't all be in the physical pull you feel toward someone.

"My advice," Joy interrupts my raging thoughts. "If you're really that torn, talk to Gavin. Feel things out. See where he stands. I can see in the way you speak his name that he has a hold on you. But I also get your reservations about not wanting to throw away what you could have with Bryan over a guy who may or may not want more from you."

"So what are you suggesting? That I just show up wherever he is and demand to know what his intentions are with me? Cause that's not completely desperate or anything." I drop my head into my hands on a frustrated growl.

"All I'm saying is give it time. You don't have to figure it out today. The answer may find you when you least expect it. You can't force these things, no matter how badly you may want to. I know how desperately you need to control this situation, but some things are simply beyond our ability to control."

"Easier said than done," I whine, looking back up to meet her gaze.

"Find the one that speaks to your soul. When you've made your choice, you'll know it. It won't even be a choice anymore."

"God, who are you and what have you done with Joy? Here I expected some off the wall advice like— like sleep with them both and decide which one's dick you like better." I let out on a frustrated groan.

"Well you've already slept with them both," she reminds me, laughing when I give her an evil glare across the table. "I mean, sleep with both of them and find out which one's dick you like better." She smiles widely. "Better?"

"Not at all," I laugh, feeling no better about my situation.

"Well when you do, you be sure to call

me. And if you need me to check them both out and tell you which one I'd pick, I'd be happy to do that, too." She smiles wickedly. "Does whose dick *I* like better count?"

"Don't be gross." I shake my head, her comment pulling the first real laugh from me in days.

"There she is." She smiles, leaning forward to lay a brief kiss to the top of my head before pushing into a full stand. "I have to go. Maria hates when I'm late." She winks. "Call me."

"I will," I agree, throwing her a small wave as she spins around and walks away.

Knowing I need to get some shopping done to prepare for my upcoming semester which starts in two days, I push into a stand, throwing my long pea coat over my shoulders before grabbing my phone from the table. I no more than get my fingers closed around it when it buzzes to life in my hand, an unknown number dancing across the screen.

I immediately hit ignore. I make it a habit to send any number I don't recognize to voicemail. Sliding it into my jacket pocket, it vibrates again just seconds after I step out onto the sidewalk.

Same number.

"Seriously?" I mutter to myself, once again hitting the ignore button.

"You know, I don't much like being sent

to voicemail." A familiar voice washes over me.

I look up to see Gavin leaning against his truck which is parked on the street directly in front of the sandwich shop.

I suck in a ragged breath at the sight of him. His dark hair is hidden beneath a black beanie. His muscular body accented by a pair of dark jeans and a gray shirt that is only partly visible underneath his black jacket.

"What are you doing here?" The question is off my lips before I've even fully comprehended that he's here.

"I was having lunch with my sister." He points to the little Chinese restaurant to the right of the deli.

"And you just happened to know I was here, how?" I question, not able to chalk this up to coincidence.

"Because I saw you through the window." He points through the large bay window that gives a clear view of the inside of the deli and its patrons.

"How did you get my number?" I bounce to the next question.

"Stole it out of Decklan's phone." He smiles like he's really proud of himself for that one.

"Well, maybe you should have gotten the hint the first time I sent you to voicemail." I shove my phone into my pocket and set off down the sidewalk, knowing he will follow me.

Sure enough, within moments he steps up next to me, matching me stride for stride.

"Do you mind?" I throw him an annoyed glance.

"Not at all." He smiles.

"What do you want?" I stop abruptly, causing a woman walking hand in hand with a small child to sidestep to get past me.

"Now is that any way to talk to a friend?" His lopsided smile may be enough to distract my eyes, but it's not enough to melt my resolve.

"We're not friends." I act bored by this exchange.

"Well, now my feelings are hurt." He huffs, prompting a laugh to bubble in my throat.

"You're really something else, you know that?" I shake my head, not able to rid the smile that has crept its way onto my face.

"What are you doing now?" He's like a curious child playing twenty questions.

"I have a few things to pick up from the store. Anything else you need to know?"

"Want some company?" His offer catches me off guard.

"You want to come to the store with me?" I hit him with a curious look.

"Not really," he answers on a laugh, his cheeks starting to turn red from the cold. "But

I do want to spend time with you. So what store are we going to?"

"You have got to be kidding me right now?" I spin around and take off walking again, trying to ignore the fact that he's still directly by my side.

The fates must find some humor in my discomfort because for the life of me I can't figure out why I keep ending up in these ridiculous situations.

Chapter Seven

Gavin

Harlee tries to act like she's annoyed that I chose to follow her into the secondhand bookstore, but the sideways glances she keeps throwing in my direction tell me she's anything but annoyed.

I didn't actually expect my little play on her on New Year's to have such an effect, but it's clear that I have definitely ruffled her feathers a bit. I like that she's agitated. I like that she's frustrated. It will make fucking her again that much more satisfying. Just the thought of her taking out her frustrations on my back with her nails causes my dick to spring to life.

Down boy.

"So what are we looking for?" I shove an old worn book back onto the shelf before turning toward Harlee who pretends not to hear me.

"What are you doing?" She finally spins toward me, tucking the book in her hand under her arm.

"Apparently, I'm shopping for used books," I say, a smile creeping across my face.

"No. I mean what are you really doing? You're not a student. You clearly have no need for used textbooks. You're here to rile me up. Why?" She narrows her eyes at me.

"I'm just catching up with a friend." I shrug casually, picking up another book off the shelf.

"Bullshit." She rips the book from my hand, pulling my gaze back toward her. "We aren't friends, so why are you torturing me?"

"I didn't realize I was." Again I keep my tone light and casual.

Her nostrils flare slightly as a frustrated growl breaks from her lips. "Go away, Gavin," she bites, spinning around as she stomps toward the back of the store.

"Is that what you really want?" I ask, stepping up behind her.

"If your plan is to see how far you can push me with your little games until I finally lose it, you've just about succeeded."

"Hey." I grab her shoulder, spinning her toward me. "I'm sorry." All the playfulness is gone this time. "I'm not trying to play games with you."

"No?" she questions. "Because it sure feels like that's exactly what you're doing."

"Fuck." I sigh.

Gripping the bridge of my nose between two fingers, I take a deep inhale. "I don't know what I'm doing anymore," I admit, dropping my hand away. "You make me fucking crazy."

"I make you crazy?" she bites. "How the hell do you think you make me feel? One minute you're all over me, the next it's like I don't exist. Back and forth we go in this endless cycle. I'm starting to think this is fun for you."

"It isn't. You just... Fuck, Harlee, I can't stop thinking about you."

I can see the surprise that flashes across her face for the briefest moment but it's quickly replaced by anger.

"Well that's too fucking bad, isn't it? You should have thought about that after you blew me off and then treated me the way you did at the cemetery. Let's not forget the bullshit you pulled at the New Year's Eve party either."

"Are you really mad that I kissed you that night, or are you just mad that you liked it?" I take a commanding step toward her.

"I'm mad that you wait until I am dating

someone else, who I really like by the way, to decide you actually want to have something to do with me." She doesn't pull away when I reach for her hand, pulling it into mine.

"If you liked him that much, you wouldn't have let me kiss you in the first place." I lean in, our faces now so close that a mere two inches separates the distance between us.

It doesn't matter that we're standing in the middle of an old, musty bookstore. It doesn't matter that moments ago she was on the verge of slapping me. It doesn't matter that she's seeing someone who isn't me.

All that matters is the way I feel her hand tremble in mine as I lean down and press my mouth to hers.

It's the softest swipe of my lips against hers, but it does the trick. I can physically feel her resolve melt away. She lets out a small whimper, clearly wanting more. Wrapping my arm around her waist, I settle my hand against the small of her back. Pulling her firmly against me, I deepen the kiss, my clear arousal apparent as it presses into her stomach.

"Gavin, please." She pants as I trail my tongue between the seam of her lips.

"I want you." I grind my erection harder against her. "I want to feel you." I suck her bottom lip into my mouth before slowly pulling away. "Is that clear enough for you?"

She sways slightly, clearly off balance. The realization that I did this to her instantly brings a smile to my face. I've got her. Even if she doesn't want to admit it just yet, I know it.

"Now hurry the fuck up," I growl, kissing her forehead before spinning and walking away, leaving her standing in the middle of the bookstore still completely confused about what the hell just happened.

It's less than fifteen minutes before she finally emerges from the store, a large plastic bag dangling from her fingers. The moment her eyes spot me they widen. She clearly was not expecting me to still be here waiting for her.

"I thought you left." I can see the glimmer of relief in her eyes despite the fact that she tries to act completely unaffected.

"It seemed as though I was more of a distraction than anything." I tilt my head toward the store. "I figured you could use a minute to get the stuff you needed."

"O-k-a-y," she draws out, turning left to head back in the direction we came.

"When do your classes start back up?" I try to make casual conversation.

It's clear that I've pushed my luck with her. Maybe it's time I work on actually showing her why she shouldn't hate my guts.

"Tuesday." She keeps her eyes focused forward.

"I don't think you've ever mentioned what you're studying." I pry, genuinely curious to learn more about this girl.

"Probably because you've never cared to ask." A small smile plays on her mouth and I can tell she rather enjoys busting my balls.

"Fair enough. So, what are you studying?" I ask when she makes no attempt to offer the information.

"Substance abuse counseling," she says, keeping her gaze focused in front of her.

"Really? Any particular reason?"

"Just seems like a good way to be able to help people." She flashes her hazel eyes at me for the briefest moment, and I swear I see a hint of sadness behind them.

I'm starting to understand that there is much more to this girl than I originally thought.

"Don't want to talk about it. Accepted." I nudge her shoulder with mine. "But for the record, I'm a pretty good listener if given the chance."

"For some reason I find that hard to believe," she jabs again.

"Ouch," I say, acting as if she's physically wounded me. "That hurts."

"Shut up," she laughs, shaking her head as she meets my gaze again.

"I like your laugh." I reach out, wrapping my fingers around hers.

It surprises me that she allows me to hold her hand, but it surprises me even more how much I enjoy doing it.

"Almost as much I like the sound of you moaning," I tack on, raising my eyebrows up and down suggestively.

"Oh my god. You really are something else." She laughs again, turning her face in an attempt to hide her blush.

"What are you doing Friday night?" I ask, turning my gaze forward.

"I'm not sure yet, why?"

"A few of us are getting together for dinner. Nothing fancy. Just a casual sit down with some friends. You interested?"

"I shouldn't." She shakes her head.

"You should," I correct her. "Kimber and Decklan will be there. As will Paxton, my sister Charlie, and maybe a couple others. Come on, it'll be fun."

"Maybe another time." She once again refuses.

"You know, it's not illegal for us to actually hang out," I remind her.

"Gavin, I have a boyfriend." She hits me with a look that says she wishes she didn't.

"You don't need to remind me. I am perfectly aware of the *boy* you insist on claiming is your boyfriend."

"He *is* my boyfriend," she objects. "We've been dating exclusively for nearly a month now."

"Have you now?" I hold up our entwined hands, tightening my grip when she starts to pull away. "It didn't seem so exclusive when you were kissing me."

"I..." she starts, but I cut her off.

"Look, you're seeing someone, I get it. That doesn't mean I have to like it or that I'm just going to accept it. It just means I'm going to have to try that much harder to make sure it doesn't work out."

The shock that registers on her face is both fucking adorable and infuriating. What the fuck does she think I'm doing here? I thought I'd made it pretty clear that she's what I want. Maybe I haven't been clear enough.

"Well you're wasting your time," she says before tugging her hand out of mine.

Coming to an abrupt halt, she spins toward me, clearly ready to give me an earful. But before she can get anything out, my hands are on her face, cupping her cold cheeks against my palms as I drop my lips to hers. As much as she tries to fight this, her reaction to my kiss gives her away. It's soft and brief, but once again I feel like it makes my point. Slowly pulling away, I put only a few inches of distance between us.

"You can pretend all you want, Harlee. But what you really want couldn't be clearer. So let me be equally as clear. I want you. And when I want something, I get it." I give her a cocky smile, letting my hands fall from her face before sidestepping past her.

She opens her mouth like she's about to argue but then closes it again, something obviously catching her attention. Panic flashes across her flushed face before she eventually plasters on a fake smile and straightens her shoulders. It isn't until I follow her line of sight that I see the douche bag she's dating heading toward us, his eyes bouncing between the two of us.

"Hey." She smiles when he steps up directly in front of her.

"Hey." He leans forward, casually dropping a kiss to her forehead.

The action makes me want to shove his fucking ass through the window of the flower shop next to us. But given the relief that seems to wash over Harlee, I refrain from doing anything to ruffle his feathers. It's clear he didn't see our little interaction just moments prior, though a part of me wishes he had.

"I tried calling you," he continues, his focus firmly on her.

"Oh sorry. I had lunch with Joy and then had to run to the bookstore." She holds up the bag in her hand. "I ran into Gavin along the way." She flips her eyes to me, the small glimmer of panic evident in her stare.

She watches me warily, clearly very

concerned about what I might do or say. I throw her a knowing smile and then turn toward the *boy*.

"Gavin Porter." I extend my hand to him. "I don't believe we've officially met. You came to my bar on New Year's."

"The business partner." He connects the dots, giving my hand a brief shake before pulling back. "I had the pleasure of meeting Decklan a few days ago."

"Well I don't know how much of a pleasure meeting that asshat is, but I'll tell him you said so." He laughs at my obvious joking.

"Quite a place you guys have over there. I appreciate you guys showing us such a great time." He seems completely at ease with me which bothers me more than it should.

The last thing I want him to feel in my presence is comfortable.

"Glad you enjoyed yourself." I nod.

"Oh we did, didn't we, babe." He drops an arm over Harlee's shoulder. The action causes me to twitch slightly.

"We did," she confirms, wrapping her arm around his waist as if to make a point about my earlier statement.

"You want to go grab some coffee?" He turns his attention back to Harlee, tucking a long strand of light blonde hair behind her ear. His hand lingers on the side of her face just a fraction too long, and I have to shove my hands into my pockets to keep myself from pushing him off of her.

"Sure." She gives him a sweet smile, pushing up to lay a kiss to his jaw.

Now who's toying with whom?

"Gavin, you're welcome to join us." Bryan turns back to me.

The laid back surfer thing he has going on for whatever reason grates on me. Probably because if not for the woman standing between us, I might actually like the cock sucker.

Regardless, I have no desire to sit and watch him hang all over Harlee. Of course, the thought of what might happen if I'm not there is even worse.

"No. No thanks." I shake my head, not missing the relief that flashes across Harlee's face. "It was good seeing you again, Harlee," I say, meeting her eyes for a brief moment. "Nice meeting you, man." I nod toward Bryan.

"You, too," he calls after me as I take off down the sidewalk back toward my truck.

Anger spirals through me. It takes everything I have not to turn around and force her to come with me. That little shit display she put on was the weakest attempt I have ever seen at trying to deter me from pursuing her.

If anything, she has made this an even

more interesting little game we seem to be playing now. She wants to dangle her little boy in front of me? She thinks that's gonna scare me off? She has no fucking clue who the hell she's dealing with.

Challenge accepted.

Chapter Eight

Harlee

"Why am I doing this?" I stare at my reflection, wondering what on earth could have possessed me to agree to Kimber's invitation for dinner when I had already declined Gavin's.

I catch my hazel eyes in the floor length mirror and study myself for a long moment. As much as I try to convince myself that the only reason I am doing this is because Kimber asked me to, I know that's not the case. Just like with New Year's, a part of me is one hundred percent aware that my reasoning has much more to do with a handsome cocky bar owner than it does my friend.

No matter how much I tell myself what a horrible idea this is, I'm determined to prove to myself that I can exist in a world where Gavin Porter is nothing more than my friend's boyfriend's best friend.

I've made my choice. Bryan. He's sweet and kind, fun and charming. He doesn't send me soaring on the emotional rollercoaster that Gavin does. He doesn't play games or purposely try to rile me up to see how far he can push me. He wants nothing more from me than *me*. I'd be an idiot to throw all that away for a man like Gavin Porter.

Taking a deep breath, I straighten the hem of my black sweater dress before taking a step back to inspect the rest of my attire; dark gray leggings partnered with two-inch black heels. It's a cute outfit but casual enough that it doesn't look like I'm trying too hard. This is exactly the type of outfit a girl wears out to a casual dinner with friends which is precisely why I picked it.

I decided to leave my long light blonde hair hanging down my back in loose curls and kept my makeup light; limiting myself to nude colors, a light coating of mascara, and clear lip gloss. I'm trying my best not to try too hard and yet I still can't help but feel like trying too hard is exactly what I'm doing.

"You ready? Car's here." Kimber pulls my attention to where she's standing next to the door, a small clutch purse in her hand.

I hadn't even realized she was ready yet, but it's clear to see she's been waiting on me for at least a couple minutes now. I scan my eyes down her short, slender frame. Per usual, she looks amazing. Like me she's wearing a long sweater, only hers is blue and gray striped and paired with tight dark skinny jeans.

"Ready." I sigh, grabbing my wristlet purse from the dresser before crossing the space toward her. "Your hair looks really cute like that," I say, reaching out to trail my fingers through the ends of her blonde waves which are tied off in a loose side pony.

"You don't think I look like I'm twelve?" She crinkles her nose.

"Not even a little." I laugh, pulling open the door to our dorm room before following her out into the hallway.

"Thank you again for coming. As much as I love Decklan's friends, I always get nervous whenever we do a group function. It makes me feel better knowing at least one person there is on my side." She throws me a sideways smile before pushing her way outside.

I immediately wrap my arms around myself, a crisp breeze blowing across my face the moment we step out into the chilly evening air. I probably should have thought to wear a coat but honestly, I hate lugging one around unless I know I'm going to be outside for any real length of time.

Thankfully, it doesn't take us long to reach the cab sitting on the curb just a few feet from the sidewalk. It isn't until we slide into the back that I turn my attention back to Kimber.

"Why did Decklan not pick you up?" I ask.

"Because it's freezing on his motorcycle for one. I don't know how he manages to ride that thing twelve months a year." She shivers just thinking about it. "Besides, did you expect him to fit both of us on the back?" she laughs.

"I guess I didn't think about that," I admit.

"The restaurant is local, so it cost next to nothing to pay a cab. I guess Gavin didn't want Charlie to have to travel all the way to Portland so everyone is coming down this way. I would have suggested he pick us up, but he's already giving Paxton and Charlie a ride so it's doubtful they could have squeezed us into his truck, too."

I don't know why I never thought to ask where we were going. The fact that we are going somewhere in Eugene is news to me. I just assumed we'd be driving to Portland. My stomach twists slightly at the thought of being in a location where Bryan might walk in.

I'm just going out with friends, I remind myself. Bryan knows I'm having dinner with Kimber and a few others. I'm not doing anything wrong. But if that's the case, why do I already feel so damn guilty?

"Did you tell Gavin I was coming with you?" I ask, pulling Kimber's attention from looking out the window, back to me.

"I told Decklan. Not sure if he mentioned it or not. Why do you ask?" She hits me with suspicious eyes.

"Just wondering. He invited me to come with you guys; I told you that. But at the time I didn't think I'd be able to, so I told him I couldn't."

Up to this point, I have divulged very little about my situation with Gavin to Kimber. I don't want to put her in an awkward position where she's stuck between the two of us. To be completely honest, I'm not really sure how I would explain what's going on anyway. It's all so random and confusing.

She knows we talked New Year's, though I left out the earth-bending kiss. She also knows I ran into him on Sunday after having lunch with Joy but again, I didn't tell her anything about him kissing me. As far as I've told her, we have put aside the fact that we slept together a couple months ago and have decided to try to be friends.

"Gotcha. Well, either way, I'm sure it's

fine." She gives me a warm smile before turning her attention back out the window. She seems distracted for some reason. She keeps knotting her hands in her lap like she's nervous.

I hope it doesn't have anything to do with me. A shiver of panic runs through me. What if she knows I'm lying to her? A part of me feels like she believes me. The other part feels like she knows I am full of complete and total shit. Either way, I'm sticking to my story.

I feel bad keeping secrets from Kimber. In the few months we have been roommates, we have become extremely close. She trusted me when everything went down with her and Decklan, and yet here I am shutting her out.

Just another thing to add to my list of ways that I suck.

I've told Angel everything, of course. Her advice was— no surprise here— to fuck him again and see how I feel. I tried telling her I don't need to fuck him again; I already know how I feel, but she refuses to accept that as a valid response.

Maybe I should take her advice for once...

"We're here." Kimber's voice pulls me back to the present, and I immediately shake off the lingering thought.

I look out the window just in time to see the cab pull up in front of *Ramshacks*, a hopping bar and grill not ten minutes from campus. I've been here several times before and it's a location I am extremely comfortable with. At least I have that much and not in some strange place two hours from home. This place offers me an easy escape should I need it. Not to mention, I know at least a handful of the waitresses from school.

I follow Kimber out of the car and into the restaurant, taking a deep breath before pushing my way inside. It takes a few moments for my eyes to adjust to the dim overhead lighting and I blink rapidly several times before the interior finally comes into view.

It's busy but not too bad considering it's a Friday night. Most of the booths that circle the far walls of the room are full, but there are several high-top tables around the bar that are still empty. Kimber grabs my hand and pulls me in that direction.

Before I even have a chance to react, she leads me to one of the already occupied high tops, this one a long rectangle that seats eight. I recognize Paxton first. He throws Kimber a wide smile and nods in our direction, prompting Decklan, whose back is to us, to turn.

"Hey." He gives her a jaw-dropping smile and pulls her against him. Her body disappears into his embrace, his muscular arms caging her in.

She pushes up and lays a kiss to his scruffy jaw before stepping back and giving the other two people at the table a little wave.

"Paxton you've met Harlee, yes?" She addresses the too hot for his own good musician, who hits me with a panty-melting smile.

Holy hell what is with these guys? All three of them are unbelievably good looking; Paxton, even better than I remembered. Don't even get me started on Decklan. And then Gavin... Well, I think I've made it pretty clear how irresistible that one is. Even on a good day, with a clear mind, I have trouble thinking straight in his presence.

"We have." Paxton interrupts my thoughts. "Good to see you again, Harlee." He nods.

"You too." I smile, turning to the next person Kimber starts to introduce.

"This is Gavin's cousin, Tracy." She gestures to the young brunette sitting directly across from Decklan. "Tracy, this is my roommate, Harlee."

"Nice to meet you, Tracy," I say, giving the girl a smile.

If I had to guess, I'd say she's at least a couple years younger than I am. There's an innocence to her big chocolate eyes. Something that tells me she hasn't quite seen the world for the way it is just yet.

"There you are." Kimber's head snaps to the side, and I follow her sight.

The moment his face comes into view, I suck in a ragged breath. Not only because Gavin looks incredible in his dark jeans and fitted black shirt, but also because he has a gorgeous slender brunette on his arm. One that hits me with dark eyes the moment she steps up in front of me.

At first, I think she's going to hit me or something, the way she studies me for a long moment. Instead, she wraps her arms around my neck and pulls me into a tight hug.

"You must be Harlee. It's so nice to meet you," she sings, finally releasing me after a long moment.

"I... Um..." I stutter, not sure who the hell this person is.

"Charlie, leave her alone and go sit down." Gavin shoves at her playfully.

Charlie... His sister.

Relief immediately floods through me. For a moment I thought I was going to have to endure him hanging all over some beautiful brunette all night. I hate that the thought even bothers me, but it does. Knowing she's his sister brings a whole new level of panic to the surface.

How does she know about me? Has he talked to her about us? About me? What has he said? Certainly, given the fact that she hugged me, he must have told her something. Why would he tell his sister about me?

The questions flood my mind as I watch Charlie cross around the table and slide into the stool next to Paxton. Now that I really look at her, it's clear she's related to Gavin. They have the same dark hair, the same big eyes— despite the fact that they're different colors, and the same wide, mischievous smile.

"I'm glad you changed your mind." Gavin pulls my attention back to him just as Kimber slides into the seat next to Decklan, leaving the two seats directly across from them empty.

As much as I don't want to, I know that I am going to be stuck sitting directly next to Gavin. I'm already getting lightheaded by the incredible smell radiating off of him. It's hard saying how I will feel having to endure being so close to him for the duration of dinner.

"Well, Kimber asked," I say, avoiding his gaze as I cross around the backside of the table and take the seat across from Kimber.

As I predicted, Gavin wastes no time sliding in next to me, giving me a knowing smile as he does. I hate that he thinks this is all about him. Is it that far out of the realm of possibility that I would come here for Kimber and not him?

I look down the table at the row of

people across from me. Kimber, Decklan, and Tracy all line the front side, where Charlie, Paxton, Gavin, and I occupy the other.

"Is anyone else coming?" Kimber asks the exact question I was thinking.

"No, I think this is it," Gavin answers. "We invited Mia too, but she's busy with her kids." He seems almost relieved by this fact.

I get the feeling him and his older sibling are not all that close. Though I'm sure the difference in age has something to do with it. From what Kimber has told me, which isn't all that much, Mia, who is six years older than Gavin, is not quite as laid back as the rest of the Porter family.

I turn my attention to the menu in front of me, eager to have something to focus on other than the man sitting next to me. I swear I feel his eyes on the side of my face, but I choose to ignore him as I continue to read over the menu, despite the fact that I know exactly what I want.

I order the same thing every time I come here: a club sandwich and sweet potato fries. And while usually it's one of my favorites, right now the thought of stomaching any food makes me feel half ill.

Gavin squeezes the top of my thigh causing me to jump slightly in my stool. Finally looking in his direction, I pin wide eyes on him. He laughs and then nods his head to the side. Only then do I realize the waitress standing at the edge of our table, clearly waiting for me to order my drink. How did I not even notice she was there?

"Sorry." I give her a weak smile, grateful that I have no idea who she is. "I'll take a water with lemon please," I say, feeling the goose bumps spread down my back as Gavin's hand once again settles on my leg, this time sliding upward slowly instead of grabbing me playfully.

My whole body tenses and I turn my gaze back to his face, tempted to smack off the smug smile I see there.

"Stop," I mouth, pushing his hand away.

He lets out a small chuckle, clearly not the least bit concerned about what anyone else at the table is doing.

"No," he mouths back, his gaze holding firmly to mine.

Before I can even react, I feel his hand come to a rest just above my knee. The thin material of my leggings offers no protection from the heat of his touch as it slides slowly upward once again. Every painfully slow inch it climbs, the tighter my lower belly clenches, a need forming deep inside of me. A need I know only one thing will satisfy.

When he stops just inches from my upper thigh, I relax a little. I ignore the nagging sense of disappointment I feel as I try to focus on the conversation currently taking place around the table. Something about Charlie enrolling at the University of Oregon for her last year, but I've already missed too much of what was said to really follow.

I turn my attention to Kimber, who instead of listening to Charlie, seems to be focused solely on me. She looks between Gavin and me for a long moment before a knowing smile begins to creep across her face.

She throws me a wink and then turns away, leaving me staring across the table at her in complete confusion. What is it that she saw that prompted her reaction? Am I that transparent that without any action she can read me so easily?

I'm still trying to sort through all of this when I feel Gavin's grip tighten on my thigh. I flick my eyes toward him, my frustration starting to mount. I expect to see him staring at me with teasing eyes and a cocky smile; what I find instead is so much worse.

Blue, lust-filled eyes settle on mine just moments before I feel his warm hand cup my sex, causing me to let out a slow, shaky breath. I want to turn away, break the contact, but I can't seem to muster it.

At this moment, all I want is him. I want to feel his hand bare against my most sensitive flesh and not against the barrier of my pants. I want to feel his lips hot against my neck, my breasts, lighting up my entire body.

I want all of these things and yet none of them at all. Because I know that succumbing to such wants will only make things that much worse. With every touch, I want another. With every kiss, I crave more. I am stuck in this endless battle of head versus heart, and I can feel both teetering beneath the undeniable spark this man lights inside of me.

Chapter Nine

<u>Harlee</u>

"Will you excuse me for a moment?" I say to no one in particular, sliding out of my stool in an effort to get away from Gavin's consuming touch.

"Ladies," I mouth to Kimber who nods and turns her attention back to Decklan, who is currently having a conversation with Paxton that I have not been able to concentrate on long enough to follow.

I ignore the heat that burns across my back where I'm sure Gavin's eyes are watching me as I cross around the bar and disappear down the long hallway that houses the bathrooms.

Stepping inside the ladies room, I immediately cross to the sink. Resting my palms on either side, I take a deep breath, finally peering up at my reflection in the mirror. My cheeks are flushed and a small layer of perspiration has formed along my hair line. My god, what is this man doing to me?

Grabbing a paper towel, I quickly turn on the cold water, dampening the cloth. Flipping the water off, I ring out the excess liquid from the towel before blotting it across my forehead, trying to cool myself down despite the fact that it's not even the least bit warm in the restaurant. If anything it's cooler than I normally would prefer.

"Get yourself together," I say to my reflection, taking several deep breaths before tossing the towel in the trash can.

I spin toward the door and exit. The moment I emerge on the other side, a hand closes down around my forearm, pulling me to the side.

"What the..." I don't get the rest of my sentence out. Warm lips settle over mine, silencing my voice. My entire body erupts in a chaos of prickles and butterflies.

"I've wanted to do that all night," Gavin breathes against my mouth before deepening the kiss.

It's like my body is operating on auto-pilot, my mind too clouded to consciously take any ownership of my actions. I don't stop him when his tongue slides into my mouth. I don't stop him when his hands settle on my hips, forcing his arousal to press firmly against my stomach. I don't stop him even though I know that is exactly what I should do.

It isn't until I hear a throat clear that the real world seems to return, and I remember where the hell I am and what I'm doing. Gavin immediately breaks away from my mouth, our heads turning toward the noise in unison.

My heart leaps into my throat when I see a very amused Kimber standing just feet from us, her arms crossed in front of her chest, a large smile lighting up her entire face.

"Food's here," she says, focusing her gaze on me as I slide out of Gavin's embrace. "You've been gone for a while. I wanted to make sure everything was okay." She looks behind me to Gavin. "I see you're just fine." She smiles, spinning around without another word.

I follow her back to the table in silence, noticing immediately that Gavin chooses to hang back and not come with us. I avoid Decklan's gaze as I slide into my stool. Looking down at the food in front of me, I reach for the ketchup like nothing out of the ordinary is going on.

I feel Gavin reappear at the table moments later, but I don't look in his direction right away. I need a few minutes to process, to figure out what the hell just happened before I find myself sucked back into the trance he seems to put me in.

I keep my focus on my food, forcing down one sweet potato fry at a time despite the fact that each one I eat seems to stick in my throat and threatens to come back up. Gavin doesn't touch me again. I think he knows I need a little space, and I'm thankful he's not pushing it.

I turn my attention to Kimber when I hear her whisper arguing with Decklan who appears to be anything but angry. In fact, he seems happy. Really happy. He ignores Kimber's attempts to deter him from whatever it is he's about to do, turning his attention to everyone at the table.

"Since we have all of you here, I'd like to make an announcement," Decklan starts, ignoring Kimber's attempts to silence him. "This is not how we planned to tell you all, but it seems easier this way since we're all together." He drops his arm around Kimber's shoulder and proudly tucks her into him. "I've asked Kimber to marry me."

His announcement causes more than one person at the table to gasp in surprise and poor Tracy looks suddenly very ill. I don't know why, but it seems like no one saw this coming. Obviously, they know Decklan much better than I do because I'm not the least bit surprised by this news.

"Obviously, I said yes," Kimber huffs, giving Decklan an aggravated look, which immediately turns into a smile when he crinkles his nose playfully at her.

He drops a sweet kiss to her mouth, prompting an even larger smile from her when he pulls his face away.

"I love you," he mouths, ignoring the congratulations and hoots of celebration that now sound around the table.

This is what changed me. Witnessing the type of love Decklan and Kimber have for each other has only intensified my need to be loved like that. Before they got together, I was happy in my ignorance. I thought being free to hook up and do whatever I wanted to do was what would make me happy.

Now I see how wrong I was. What would make me happy is to find someone who looks at me the way Decklan looks at Kimber. I flip my eyes hesitantly to Gavin whose hand closes down around mine underneath the table even though his eyes remain focused on his best friend.

It's almost like he can sense the sadness and yet utter elation that is seeping through me all at the same time.

"I think you can put your ring on now." Decklan nudges Kimber's shoulder with his, clearly very anxious to show the world just who she belongs to.

She grins up at him before grabbing her clutch purse from the table. Moments later she is pulling out a radiant cut halo ring with a light pink diamond perched in the center. It's probably the most beautiful ring I've ever seen. The style and color fit Kimber perfectly; beautiful, elegant, one of a kind.

"We're going to wait a while." Kimber immediately turns her gaze to me as she slides the ring onto her finger. "I'm not moving out on you or anything," she promises, which is actually quite a relief. I can't even begin to imagine what college would be like without having Kimber as my roommate.

"We were thinking maybe next year," Decklan continues for her.

"We still have a lot of details to figure out," she adds, smiling up at her fiancée.

Fiancée... It's odd to think about.

"Well this calls for a toast," Gavin announces after several long moments.

His hand finally releases mine as he stands, holding up his bottle of beer.

"To Decklan and Kimber." The smile on his face literally takes my breath away. I don't think I have ever seen a more beautiful man up close.

"Deck, you aren't just my best friend, you're my brother," He continues. "I couldn't be happier for you right now man. Kimber." He turns his attention to my teary-eyed friend. "You gave him peace. Something I never thought he'd find. I'll never be able to truly thank you for that. Take care of him."

"Here. Here," Paxton chimes in, standing to raise his beer bottle as well. Everyone else at the table follows suit, raising their glasses to toast Kimber and Decklan.

Once everyone has settled back into their seats and the initial shock of their announcement seems to have worn off, the conversation once again flows freely around the table.

"It's ours," Decklan answers simply when Charlie presses to find out how he proposed. "Our memory. Something just for us." He winks down at Kimber before turning back to Charlie who seems almost impressed with his response.

She catches Paxton's gaze as she turns away from Decklan, and I can't help but feel like I see something in their exchange. I keep my eyes on them for several more seconds before I realize it must have just been in my head. The two seem completely at ease and normal, though a part of me can't help but wonder if that's not an act for their current audience.

I decide it's none of my business, turning my head away. That's when I realize

Gavin is staring at me. Not just *looking* at me but *staring*. His eyes are locked on my face and his forehead is scrunched together like he's in deep thought.

When I catch his gaze he instantly snaps out of it, giving me a warm smile before turning away. Making a grab for his beer bottle, he drains the contents in one long gulp and then turns back toward me.

"You want to get out of here?" He keeps his voice low enough that no one else at the table can hear what he's saying, his blue eyes locked on mine.

"I can't," I answer just as quietly, shaking my head.

"Yes you can," he challenges.

I flick my eyes to Kimber who nods when Decklan whispers something to her and then turns toward me.

"Will you be okay if I go back to Portland with Decklan tonight?" she asks, clearly not needing my permission but just wanting to be considerate since we came here together.

I ignore the fact that just two seconds prior Gavin proposed I leave with him. Kimber was my excuse not to. I can already feel the panic start to creep up my spine like a swarm of tiny spiders climbing across my flesh.

"Of course," I say like it should be obvious. "I can catch a cab back to the dorm."

"I'll take you back," Gavin offers, pulling my attention back to him.

"You don't have room for me, do you?" I struggle to find an excuse, remembering Kimber said Paxton and Charlie were riding with Gavin.

"Paxton drove separately. I can drop Charlie at the house and then take you home," he says, causing my stomach to double over in a flutter of nervousness.

"Paxton can run me home," Charlie interjects, turning to Paxton who immediately nods like it's not a problem.

"There, it's settled." Gavin hits me with a wide, mischievous smile.

"Awesome." I try to hide the sarcasm that drips from my voice.

The last thing I want is to be stuck alone with Gavin. I wish I could say I trust myself enough to resist him, but if I'm being honest I don't. I know the effect he has on me. I know the way he makes me feel and the way my entire mind seems to turn to mush when he kisses me.

These are the thoughts that plague my mind for the remainder of dinner. By the time we exit the restaurant a half an hour later, my anxiousness has only intensified. I feel like a bundle of nerves that's about to split apart and float off in a million different directions.

"Thanks again for taking her home,

Gavin." Kimber smiles up at him before pulling me into a brief hug. "Be good," she whispers, meeting me with a knowing smile when she releases me.

"Don't freeze to death," I tease, watching her zip her coat and pull her gloves on.

"No promises," she laughs, taking the helmet Decklan hands to her.

"Be safe," I say, throwing her and Decklan one last small wave before turning to follow Gavin toward the opposite side of the parking lot.

I open my mouth to speak several times during the short walk toward Gavin's truck, but by the time we reach it I still haven't managed to get even one word out. I don't know what to say and honestly, I'm not sure any of it would make a difference.

"Thank you." I muster a small nod as Gavin pulls the passenger door of the truck open and gestures for me to climb inside.

He lets out a small chuckle, clearly enjoying the fact that he's making me squirm. I'm not really sure why I'm so nervous. Then again, I think I know exactly why I am at the same time.

"You know." He grabs the seat belt and stretches it across my waist. "I don't bite." His words dance across my face as he latches the buckle. "There." He smiles.

"You realize I can buckle my own seat

belt." I fake annoyance even though the protective gesture makes my heart flutter inside my chest.

"Good for you." His smile turns wicked as he steps back and slams the door shut.

Within seconds he's climbing into the driver's side and snapping his own seatbelt before firing the engine to life. He slowly pulls from the parking lot, purposely keeping his focus on the road as he avoids meeting my gaze.

After a few long moments of silence, I feel like my head might explode if I don't say something. I blurt the first thing that comes to mind.

"You didn't seem surprised about Decklan and Kimber's announcement," I observe, keeping my eyes locked out the window.

"That's because I already knew."

"How long have you known?" I ask, a little offended that I was left out of the loop.

"I went with him to get the ring," he answers flatly.

"And how long ago was that?" I ask, realizing that in the surprise of hearing the marriage news, I never actually got around to asking when he had proposed.

"Last week."

"Last week?" I flip my gaze to him. "You mean you knew on Tuesday and you never said anything?" I gape at him in disbelief.

"He hadn't asked her yet." He chuckles lightly. "I wasn't about to ruin his proposal before he even got a chance to make it."

"I guess that makes sense," I agree, knowing I would have done the same thing. "But you still could have said something. It's not like I would've run off to tell Kimber or anything."

"Not a chance I was willing to take. Not when it wasn't my shit to tell." He shrugs, meeting my eyes for a brief moment before flipping them back toward the road.

Seconds later he pulls the truck into a vacant spot outside of my dorm building and kills the engine. I immediately reach to unbuckle my seatbelt, anxious to escape the confines of this vehicle. Before I can even get my hand to the latch, Gavin stops me. His fingers close down around my forearm, pulling my gaze up to his.

"Just where do you think you're going?" He gives me a wicked smile, his eyes growing impossibly dark.

My stomach does a flip for the millionth time this evening and I suck in a ragged inhale, determined not to let this man cloud my better judgment. The judgment that tells me sleeping with him would be about the worst thing I could do. Not just to Bryan but myself as well.

I don't know if I can walk away from Gavin a second time. I don't know that I even want to. What I do want is to not be put in the position to make that choice at all.

Gavin unlatches his seatbelt and slides across the bench seat until he's right next to me, his breath hot on my cheek as I try to look anywhere but into his eyes. The eyes that suck me in and blind me from everything but the gorgeous man they belong to.

"Look at me, Harlee," he commands, his voice causing a shiver to run down my back.

"No." The word is weak and barely breaks the surface.

"Look at me," he repeats, his hand closing down on my chin as he pulls my face toward him.

When my eyes find his face, I expect to see humor, a teasing smile telling me he knows he's got me. What I see instead takes my breath away. It catches in my throat, making it impossible for my lungs to suck in the air they feel so desperate for.

I can't grasp what the look means or even begin to understand it. All I know is that something has shifted. This is no longer funny to him. It's no longer a game. He wants me and not because he knows he can have me.

And now he's got me. Before his face lowers to mine. Before his lips brush gently against my mouth. Before his hand unlatches my seatbelt and his strong arms pull me against his rock hard torso.

He had me in that one look.

Chapter Ten

Gavin

"Gavin." Her whispered word against my lips is enough to make my hunger for her damn near unbearable.

I suck her bottom lip into my mouth, loving the way it coaxes a light groan from the back of her throat.

"Please," she whimpers, begging me.

I tighten my grip on her waist, hoisting her into my lap. She rests both her knees on either side of me, her mess of hair hanging down around us, tickling my face. Wrapping my hand around the back of her neck, I pull her face back down to mine, running my tongue along the seam of her lips before plunging it into her mouth.

She grinds down on my erection, another moan escaping when she realizes just how badly I want her.

All I want is to feel her tight around me, to show her exactly why she belongs right here and not with that douche she calls a boyfriend. She's mine now, whether she knows it or not.

There's no way in fuck I am letting her go again.

Grabbing the hem of her dress, I break away from her mouth just long enough to slide it over her head before tossing it onto the floorboard of the truck. I don't worry about anyone seeing us, given that it's pitch black outside and the windows are completely fogged.

I doubt Harlee even cares at this point.

Her fingers dig into the back of my hair and she slams her mouth back down onto mine, her entire body rigid with want and need. The thought that I'm the one doing this to her brings out an almost animalistic need to claim her.

Pushing up, I spin, dropping her onto her back against the seat of the truck. Grabbing the waistband of her pants, I have them and her panties down before she has even processed my action.

I am so desperate to get inside of her; my hands are shaking by the time I unlatch my belt and jeans. Retrieving a condom from the glove box of the truck, I roll it down onto my cock, which is so hard it's borderline painful, before spreading Harlee's legs wider.

I settle in between them, her thighs squeezing tightly against my hips as I line my erection at her entrance. With one last look into her lust filled eyes, I push forward, groaning out when the tightness of her settles around me.

She feels so good. So fucking good.

"This isn't going to last long, baby," I breathe against her mouth before dropping a heated kiss to her lips. "You feel so fucking good around me." I groan, pulling almost completely out of her before plunging back in.

Placing my hands on the door behind her, I throw one of her legs over my shoulder, sinking into her so deeply her head rolls to the side and a deep moan sounds from her throat. I pull out and then ram in again, loving that every time I do her actions and sounds become less censored and wilder and out of control.

It isn't long before I have worked myself into a steady rhythm, pounding in and out with so much force she has to push against the door above her head to keep herself in place.

"You. Are. Mine," I grind out, my release threatening to rip through me at any moment. "Say it Harlee." I increase my speed. "Tell me you're mine," I demand.

"I'm yours," she cries moments before I feel her tighten around me.

"Fuck!" I groan, her orgasm sending me soaring over the edge. The pleasure rips through me; the feeling of her clenching around me the most fucking incredible thing in the world.

Once I'm sure I have drained every last ounce of pleasure I can from her, I collapse down on top of her, resting my head against her chest. Her heart is beating so rapidly I can feel it pounding against the side of my face.

"What the fuck are you doing to me?" I ask, loving the way her chest rises and falls beneath me as she tries to catch her breath.

"I could ask you the same question," she whispers, dropping her hands into my hair.

She runs her fingertips along my scalp, the feeling damn near lulling me to sleep despite the fact that I'm anything but tired.

****

It took everything I had in me to let Harlee leave my truck. After lying with her in my arms for almost an hour, it was nearly impossible to drive away.

The combined scents of our bodies danced around me in the cab of the truck the entire way back to Portland. You would think after a two-hour drive I wouldn't still be wearing this ridiculous ass smile, but as I pull my truck into the parking garage of my condo building, I still haven't managed to shake it.

I shove the truck into park after pulling into my assigned space, killing the engine before climbing out. Within minutes, I'm stepping out of the elevator onto the seventeenth floor, turning right as I take the hall all the way to the end. I shove my key into the door the moment I reach it.

I immediately spot Paxton, lounging in the living space that sits directly off the foyer, a beer in one hand, the television remote in the other.

"Where the fuck have you been?" He tosses the remote next to him on the black leather couch, giving up on finding anything to watch.

"With Harlee." I hang my keys on the wall before sliding off my converse.

"As in *with* Harlee?" He raises his eyebrows suggestively, taking a long drag of his beer.

"As in none of your fucking business," I huff, crossing through the living room into the kitchen-dining room combo that is separated from the living space by a half wall.

"Defensive; that's new," Paxton observes. "I didn't realize you guys were a real thing." He stands, crossing into the kitchen to grab another beer from the fridge. "Here." He slides one into my hand before coming around to face me on the other side of the half wall.

"We aren't. I mean, we weren't," I correct, not really sure what the fuck we're doing.

All I know is I want more. So much fucking more.

"Isn't she seeing someone?" He eyes me curiously.

"So what if she is?" I twist the cap off my beer and take a long swig, the cold liquid causing my eyes to water slightly as it slides down my throat.

"I didn't realize you were *that* guy," he states matter of fact.

"If you mean the kind of guy who takes what the fuck he wants no matter what stands in his way, then yes, I guess I am *that* guy," I say, not the least bit sorry for my actions.

Harlee belongs with me. Bryan is just going to have to move the fuck along. I may have been willing to share in the past, having never wanted someone the way I want Harlee, but I sure as shit am not willing to share her.

I want her all to myself. Every single fucking piece of her.

"You're really into this girl," he observes.

"I am," I admit, letting out a slow breath.

Harlee owns me. I've accepted it. There's

no point in trying to hide it from my brothers. Paxton and Deck are my family. I have no qualms about leaving all my shit out on display for them to see. I know at the end of the day I get no judgment from them.

"I'm happy for you." He takes a drink of his beer. "I'm just not sure how good of an idea it is to get attached to a girl who has another guy in her life."

"What the fuck is it to you?" I bite, taking another drink of my own beer.

"I don't give a fuck about the other dude." He holds his hands up in front of himself, misunderstanding my meaning. "I just want you to think long and hard about what you're doing. You're fucking another dude's girl. Have you considered that at the end of the day you're just the guy she's fucking and not the one she wants a real relationship with?"

"You don't know what you're talking about." I drain the rest of my beer in one long drink, dropping the empty bottle into the trash can next to me.

While I may not be willing to entertain the thought that somehow this doesn't go the way I want, I'd be lying if I said it hadn't crossed my mind at least once or twice over the last few days.

"Maybe not." He shrugs. "But I know you. And I know that I've never seen you quite so taken with someone before. I just don't want to see you get fucked over."

"I'm not some bleeding heart, pussy." I chuckle. "If she decides she'd rather be with him then good riddance." I play it off like I couldn't give a shit which couldn't be further from the truth.

I'm just not ready to let the doubt seep in just yet.

"Fair enough," Paxton laughs, changing the subject. "You heading into *Deviants* tonight?" he asks.

"Yeah. Deck's got Kimber over so I figure I'll head over and just make sure everything is running smoothly."

"Can you believe our boy is getting married?" He laughs, shaking his head like he still hasn't fully grasped the fact.

"Dude, I never thought I'd see the day," I agree.

"Now you're all balls deep over a chick, too." He gestures to me. "You fuckers are getting soft on me."

"Fuck you." I fake offense.

"I'm just kidding," he states the obvious. "I'm really happy for him. Kimber seems great."

"She really is. She has to be to put up with his emotional ass." I shake my head.

"What time are you heading to the bar?" he asks, reaching over the counter to drop his now empty bottle in the trash can.

"I'm gonna take a quick shower and then head over."

"Mind if I tag along? I'm going fucking stir crazy just sitting here." He gestures around the condo.

"Not at all. You have any luck finding a place yet?" I ask, knowing he's been looking for a couple weeks now.

"You getting tired of me already?" He acts overly offended but is clearly joking.

"You know you're welcome to stay here as long as you need," I say, clasping my hand down on his shoulder for a brief moment as I pass. "Whatever you need just let me know." I release my grasp on him.

I know how hard of a time Paxton has had since losing his mom. I don't think he's quite let go of the guilt he's carrying for how rocky of a relationship he had with her growing up.

"I appreciate that, man," he calls after me as I disappear down the hall that houses the condo's two bedrooms and bathrooms.

Slipping inside my room, which is the larger of the two, I cross the space to the attached bathroom, stripping off my clothes as I go.

I'm completely naked by the time I reach the shower, flipping the water on to let it warm up before finally stepping inside. The moment the hot liquid rains down over my back, Harlee's face flashes in front of my eyes. The way her nails scratched down the very place the water is now hitting. The way her lust-filled eyes held my gaze as I rocked on top of her. The sounds of her cries of pleasure.

Just the thought of it makes my fucking dick hard again. What I wouldn't give to have her right here with me at this very moment. The thought is fucking torture. To crave the feeling of her wrapped tightly around me and her not be anywhere close by to satisfy that craving is like a drug addict denying themselves the fix they so desperately need.

I don't know what the fuck it is about this girl that has me so wrapped up in her. I can't escape her, no matter how hard I try.

I'm fucking obsessed...

And there's not one fucking thing I can do about it.

Chapter Eleven

<u>Harlee</u>

The elevator ride up to Gavin's apartment feels like it lasts an eternity. I can feel every single beat of my heart, every breath my lungs take as they suck in air and let it out. I'm a wreck; a ball of nervous energy as I watch the button to the seventeenth floor finally light up and the doors slide open.

The moment my feet hit the hallway, I turn around, ready to say fuck this and spend the two-hour drive back to Eugene being pissed at myself for being such a pussy. Unfortunately, the elevator doors slide shut before I have time to react and suddenly I feel trapped like the walls are closing in around me.

Convincing myself that things between me and Gavin had to end was hard enough in itself. But now, facing the reality of actually saying those words to him has my stomach ready to rid itself of this morning's breakfast right here on the shining white tile floors.

I blame Kimber. Had she refused to give me his address when I asked, maybe I would have had time to talk myself out of this. Or maybe I should blame Joy for so willingly letting me take the Mercedes.

But then again I can't really blame them at all. I chose to put myself in this situation and now I'm choosing to get myself out of it. I know I need to get this over with, one way or another.

Crossing to the end of the hall, I stop just outside the door that reads 1723, staring at the dark distressed wood for several long seconds before finally raising my fist. Rapping lightly against the surface, I take another deep breath. I do my best to calm the shake in my knees as I await the moment I have been dreading since last night when I realized this is what had to be done.

My heart is pounding so loudly in my ears, I barely register the noise of the door opening in front of me. It isn't until intense blue eyes settle on mine that I seem to snap from my haze.

"Harlee?" Gavin's smile spreads once he's recovered from the shock of finding me standing outside his door.

"H-Hey," I stutter, momentarily distracted by the fact that he's wearing no shirt, leaving his tight, defined muscles on full display. "I'm sorry to show up like this." I try to refocus. "Can I come in for a minute?" I ask.

"Of course." He pushes the door further open and steps aside to let me pass.

The moment the interior of the condo comes into view, I can't help but be extremely surprised that this is where he lives. I expected to find a run-down bachelor pad filled with beer bottles and empty pizza boxes. Instead, I'm standing in the middle of a very stylish, open living space.

The walls are light gray, strategically designed with a few pieces of three-dimensional artwork that really gives the space character. The dark wood floors seem to run throughout the entire condo and have a distressed look just like the front door.

There's a black leather sectional couch sitting in the center of the room facing a gas fireplace, a large television mounted on the wall above it. The back wall is lined with three floor to ceiling windows that make the space feel open and airy, offering a perfect view of the city below.

"Wow," I say, finally turning back to

Gavin just as he closes the door and slides the lock into place. "This place is incredible."

"It's home." He shrugs like it's whatever. "Can I get you a drink or something?" he asks, smirking when he catches me once again eyeing his incredible body.

"No, I'm not staying long." I shake my head, turning my gaze back to his face. "I'm sorry to just show up out of the blue like this, but I need to talk to you and it's a conversation I feel is better had in person."

"O-k-a-y," he draws out, his eyebrows knitting together in confusion.

"Can we sit?" I ask, gesturing to the couch.

I hate how formal I sound, but I know the last thing I can do right now is let my guard down.

"Sure." He nods.

I take a seat on the far side of the couch, relieved when he sits on the other side so he can face me. The last thing I want is for him to get too close, especially when he's only half dressed. My mind tends to go stupid whenever this man is involved.

"What's up?" He cocks his head to the side curiously when I make no attempt to speak right away.

"We can't do this anymore, Gavin," I blurt out as I stare at the ottoman that sits directly in front of the couch, refusing to look at him. "It's not right, and I can't keep deceiving Bryan the way I have been. It's not fair to him."

"You're right." His words catch me off guard, my eyes flipping up to meet his. "It's not right because you should be with me, not him," he tacks on.

"No, that's not what I'm saying. Shit, I had this all worked out in my head," I ramble, scrambling to keep my thoughts straight. "I want to be with Bryan. I choose Bryan." I take a deep breath before once again meeting his gaze.

"I get you're scared. But you don't want him," he challenges, leaning forward to rest his elbows on his knees as his eyes burn into mine.

"Yes, I do," I argue. "He's sweet and fun, and I really like him. I can't do this anymore. I know what this is, and I can't throw away what I could potentially have with Bryan over a fling you will no doubt tire of within days."

"That's not true." His voice takes on a hardness I hadn't anticipated. "This isn't just some fucking fling. I'm not fucking playing games with you, Harlee. I thought I made that pretty clear the other night." His nostrils flare slightly causing me to shrink a bit under his heated stare.

"We both know this isn't going anywhere," I start again only to have him cut me off.

"Bullshit," he seethes, pushing into a stand.

He's across the space and pulling me to my feet before I have even processed that he's moved at all. Lifting my hand, he presses my palm against his bare chest as his face hovers just inches above mine.

"Do you feel that?" He gestures to how rapidly his heart is beating, each thud so intense it vibrates against my hand. "This is what you fucking do to me. You make me *feel*." He puts an emphasis on the word. "I don't just want your body. I want you. I want you in my life. I don't want to share you, or sneak around with you. I want you to be mine." His confession catches me off guard and I sway slightly, grabbing his forearm to steady myself.

"Gavin... I," I start but once again he doesn't let me finish.

"No." He tips my chin up, forcing me to meet his eyes. "You don't get to decide this without me. I'm just as much a part of this as you are."

"You don't know what you're saying," I finally manage to get out. "I'm sure it all sounds like fun right now, but when things get real, you're not going to want this the way you think you will."

"Don't fucking tell me what I do and do

not want. I'm not a child. Yes, this is new and it's scary as hell, but it's also the best fucking feeling I've ever had in my life," he admits, his words causing my heart to flip in my chest. "I know what I want, Harlee. I want you."

The second the words meet my ears his lips are on mine, soft at first but then more demanding. I try to resist. I try to fight against his attempt to change my mind, but it's useless. I am powerless against his advances. And what's worse, he knows it. He knows that when he kisses me, there's no way I can deny him.

My lips part involuntary and his tongue slides inside my mouth, a deep groan sounding from the back of his throat as he kisses me so deeply my body trembles against him.

He knows the moment he's got me. He can sense it in my demeanor. In the way my body goes limp against him, having no choice but to succumb to the intense want he stirs deep inside of me. I've never met a man that can command my body the way he does. I've never been with someone I couldn't walk away from. But with Gavin, all of that flies out the window.

Dipping down, he secures his hands around the back of my thighs before lifting me from the ground. I wrap my legs around his waist, securing my arms around the back of his neck as his lips fall to the base of my throat.

He nips and sucks the flesh as he slowly carries me down a dim hallway, pushing open the door at the very end. I barely register we are in a bedroom before the door slams closed and Gavin's mouth is once again on mine.

Each moment seems to happen in snaps, a timeless existence where there are no minutes or hours, but broken pieces like photographs being taken one after the other. —My back as it comes to rest on top of a soft mattress. —The eruption of goose bumps across my flesh as piece by piece it's exposed to the coolness of the room. —His lips as they trail down my chest, my stomach, nipping at my most sensitive flesh on his endless pursuit to kiss every inch of my body.

I'm so lost to the pleasure, to the feeling of being so worshipped, that by the time he rolls on a condom and settles in between my thighs, I feel like I belong to some clouded dream state rather than any actual reality.

When I feel his thick erection come to rest heavily against my pubic bone, I immediately readjust, eager to feel him inside of me. He finally enters inch by incredible inch, and I am a shameless mess of desperate need.

He lets out a deep groan as he sinks all the way inside of me, and my body takes over completely. My mind is no longer able to keep up with the demands of my lust-filled appetite.

I lift my hips to meet each of Gavin's thrusts, my body desperate and greedy for more. My nails rip at his flesh, and my teeth clamp down on his shoulder as the first orgasm washes over me within minutes, hitting me in intense waves that sends my body convulsing below him.

Just when I think I can't take another second of the pleasure that is now almost painful, I feel another orgasm start to build right behind the first.

"Gavin." His name is a plead off my lips.

"Let go, baby." He rocks back on his knees, pulling me up with him so that I am straddling his waist.

He enters me even more deeply in this position, but that's not what has my body feeling like it might split apart at any moment. It's from the feeling of his breath hot on my face. Of his hands as they lock on my hips. The look of animalistic hunger in his eyes as he grinds upward.

"Let go, baby." He rasps against my lips, sliding his tongue into my mouth. "Let go." He latches one hand down on my shoulder to hold me firmly in place as my second orgasm rips through me.

My cries of pleasure echo throughout the otherwise silent room, but it does nothing to deter me. All I hear is him. All I feel is him. All I want is him.

"Fuck," he grinds, finally succumbing to his own release as he sinks impossibly deep inside me.

He stills after several moments, dropping his face to my chest as he tries to catch his breath. Resting my chin on the top of his head, my hands work slow circles across his muscular back, neither of us ready to break the incredible connection I know we both feel.

"You told me once already that you're mine. I want to hear you say it for real this time." He speaks directly against my bare flesh, flicking his tongue against the hard bud of my nipple causing me to jump slightly.

"I don't think it's that simple," I say.

"Yes, it is." He pulls back to meet my gaze, his blue eyes so electric it causes my stomach to do a little flip. "I want you, Harlee. All to myself. I want you like this whenever I want it. I don't want to share you. Tell me you want that, too."

I wish his words didn't affect me so much. I wish I could fight off the emotion that bubbles in my throat and the excitement that flutters through my chest. He is what I want. I know that now. Hell, I've always known it.

"I want that, too," I answer honestly.

And I do. I want him more than I have ever wanted anything before in my entire life.

My only real hesitation is hurting Bryan, which is the last thing I want to do. But even as the thought crosses my mind, I know that's not entirely true. I'm also afraid to let Gavin in. I'm scared that if I do, I'll never recover when he walks away. And I truly believe eventually, he *will* walk away.

"God, what the fuck have you done to me, woman?" He hits me with a brilliant smile, pulling my face back down to his.

His lips brush against mine so sweetly that an involuntary gasp of air catches in my throat. There's something so intimate about our current position: his eyes burning into mine, his erection still deep inside of me, his lips working soft kisses across my mouth and jaw.

I can feel my heart swell inside my chest and with it comes a whole new onset of panic.

I love him.

I know it to be truer than anything else in this world. I don't know when it happened or how it happened so quickly, but as I pull back and once again meet his gaze, I know there is no denying it.

Of course, I keep my newfound revelation to myself. I don't need to add any more pressure to an already shaky situation. Because while it's easy to get lost and forget in the comfort of Gavin's arms, life is a lot more complicated outside of these four walls.

"But I need a little more time," I finally add to my previous statement after several long moments. "Can you give me that?" I ask, knowing the last thing I need is to just jump in head first without really thinking this through.

"I'll give you anything you want if it means at the end of the day that I get to call you mine." He nuzzles against my chest.

"Thank you."

I don't know if he hears my weak statement. It's more of a whisper that barely breaks the surface, but I don't make any attempt to say it again. Instead, I tighten my arms around Gavin and take a deep inhale of his incredible scent.

I may not know what the future holds. This may end up being the best thing I've ever done or my biggest mistake. All I know is right now he's all I want.

I want to commit every inch of his body to memory. I want to memorize his scent, the sound of his voice, the way his silky hair feels between my fingers. I want to remember every single detail of the moments I have with him.

Because with a man like Gavin Porter, you never know how long they'll last...

Chapter Twelve

Harlee

"So you have two sisters?" I ask, my fingers tracing lazy circles across Gavin's stomach as I lay curled into him with my head resting on his chest. "But no brothers?" I continue.

"I have two brothers," he corrects. "Decklan and Paxton."

"You know what I mean," I interject.

"I do and I answered." He chuckles lightly, his chest vibrating against my ear.

"So Mia is how old again?" I ask, just trying to make sure I have all my facts straight about him.

I'm desperate to know every detail about this man's life. I don't know why, but in a way the more I learn the closer I feel to him. And I want, no I need, to feel that closeness right now. I'm grasping at anything and everything that will calm the quake inside of me that's raging below the surface.

Fear. Love. Guilt. It all bleeds together, leaving me with a thick knot in the pit of my stomach.

"She's thirty-two," he answers on a yawn, resting his cheek against the top of my head. "And Charlie is twenty-one. While I'm at it, my mom is fifty-eight. Anything else?" He fakes annoyance.

"Shut up." I lightly smack his stomach with my hand. "Was it hard, growing up with two sisters I mean?"

"Not really. I mean, Deck and I were inseparable as kids. Hell, he practically lived at my house years before he actually moved in with us, so it always felt like I had a brother, too. What about you?"

"Only child." I try to play off the spike in my voice by quickly continuing. "I liked it better that way. No one to compete with." I laugh lightly, doing my best to mask how completely uncomfortable I am talking about my childhood.

While I'm dying to know everything about him, there are parts of myself I'm not ready to share. There are things that I haven't even told Kimber despite the fact that one of the reasons we bonded so quickly was because of our mutual dislike for our parents.

Only Angel knows everything. My mom. The way I found her. I shake away the thought, determined to not let the demons of my past ruin the otherwise perfect moment Gavin and I are sharing.

"What about your parents? Do they still live around here?" he asks, already knowing that I graduated from the same high school as him and Decklan. Of course, that was six years later so we never crossed paths.

"My mom died when I was ten," I admit, knowing that he probably already knows this or will eventually find out. It's not like it's some big secret.

"I'm so sorry." His arms tighten around me and for a moment I take comfort in his embrace, letting myself feel a small sliver of sadness for the mother I never got to have, for the one I had to bury nearly ten years ago.

"It was a long time ago." I shrug.

"And your father?" He speaks against the top of my head, his grip on me not lessening.

"He lives about an hour south of here," I answer truthfully. I just leave out the part where his residence is Oregon State Penitentiary.

"Do you see him often?" he asks, clearly not realizing that his questions are digging into a very sore subject for me.

"Not really. We aren't close," I admit.

Now that I think about it, it's been close to two years since the last time I visited my father. I hate seeing him in there. Despite the fact that he was a lowlife, deadbeat father to me and deserves to be exactly where he is, he's still my family. Seeing him in there was too hard for me, so eventually I just stopped visiting.

"Enough about me." I prop my chin up on his chest so I can peer up at him, the sight of him causing my chest to constrict.

My god, this man is beautiful.

"I want to know more about you," I add.

"I'm pretty simple." He tucks a strand of hair behind my ears. "What you see is what you get, baby." His mouth turns up in a crooked smile.

"Somehow I find that hard to believe." I roll my eyes, pushing myself up into a sitting position. "I do have a question, though."

"Shoot."

"Well, more of an observation really. You haven't smoked since I've been here."

"I quit," he replies casually.

"Seriously?" I blurt.

"Yeah, this girl I'm into kinda hates it." He shrugs, sending my heart pounding all over again.

He quit for me? The thought sends a rush of emotion flooding through me.

"Is that so?" I question playfully.

"Yeah, apparently it's really bad for me." He gives me a wide grin.

"So I've heard." I laugh, shaking my head at him before shifting toward the edge of the bed.

"Hey! Where are you going?" He grabs for me just seconds after I slide out of his reach, sitting up in bed with a playful scowl on his face.

"You can't expect to keep me prisoner here all weekend and not feed me," I whine, grabbing his vintage looking Seattle Mariners t-shirt from the floor.

I smile and take a deep inhale the moment I slide the material over my head. His scent instantly engulfs me, and I love the way it smells against my skin.

"Oh, I'll feed you alright." He gives me a wicked smile before throwing the covers back, revealing his still very naked torso.

I can't stop my eyes from trailing down the length of him. I swear there is not one inch of this man that is not complete perfection.

"Funny." I fake laugh, turning my back to him to slide my panties on. "Seriously, though," I start, my words instantly falling away when I turn and run smack dab into his hard chest.

"I wasn't trying to be funny." He dips his face down eye level with mine, his tongue darting out across his bottom lip.

At first, I think he's going to kiss me but then he backs away, a very satisfied smile pulling up the corners of his mouth. Apparently, he saw exactly the reaction he was looking for on my face.

Spinning around, he heads to the dresser that sits along the far side of the room. I can't stop my eyes from following him, focused directly on his bare ass as he rifles through drawers. He finally pulls out a plain black t-shirt and a pair of dark gray boxer briefs, sliding them on before turning back around to face me.

While I swear this man would look good wearing a garbage bag, I can't help but feel slightly disappointed that his incredible body is now hidden from my view. He must sense my disappointment because he lets out a small chuckle and shrugs.

"You had your chance." His smile is enough to make my knees shake slightly just from looking at him.

"This isn't over," I warn, spinning around and heading toward the door.

Before I can reach it, his arm snakes around my waist and he pulls my backside flush against him.

"Think again," he rasps against my ear before spinning me back around, laying a hard smack to my ass as he does. "You're not going out there in that." He points to my attire.

"Why not?" I question, looking down at myself. His shirt hangs down mid-thigh on me, so it's not like I'm not covered.

"Because I have a temporary roommate, and I am not going to give him the pleasure of seeing what belongs to me," he growls. "Pants. Now."

"God, you're bossy." I stick my tongue out at him before picking up my gray leggings off the floor and sliding them on. "Better?" I huff, crossing my arms in front of my chest.

"What will be better is when you've had a chance to eat and are back in my bed with not a fucking thing on." His eyes darken as they trail from my face to my feet and then back up again before he rips the door open and disappears down the hallway.

I can't help the huge smile that spreads across my face, my feet temporarily unable to move as the pure rush of excitement seeps through my body. I can't believe I'm here. I can't believe I've spent the last thirty-six hours in Gavin's arms, in his bed.

"Are you coming or what?" I hear him yell down the hall, snapping me out of my momentary haze.

"I'm coming. I'm coming," I call back, exiting the bedroom.

"Not the first time I've heard that come out of your mouth," he quips the moment he catches sight of me from the kitchen.

"You're really on it tonight. I bet you think you're really something special," I tease, sliding up onto the kitchen counter so that when he turns away from the refrigerator I am sitting eye level with him.

He looks at me for a long moment before crossing the short distance between us, sliding the lunch meat and condiments onto the counter before stepping in between my legs, his lips instantly finding my neck.

"Do I need to remind you just how special I am?" he asks, his fingers closing down around my hips as he pulls my body flush against his, the evidence of his arousal pressing into me.

I let out a small gasp before wrapping my hands around the back of his neck and pulling his face up to meet mine. "I think you might need to," I challenge, pressing my lips firmly against his.

He immediately deepens the kiss, his tongue sliding against mine hungrily like we haven't just spent the last several hours devouring one and another. I slide my hands down his back, pulling him even tighter against my body, wanting nothing more than to feel him inside of me right here and now.

"I'm going to fuck you, Harlee. Right here on this fucking counter." He nips at my earlobe, coaxing a small groan of pleasure from my mouth.

His grip on my hips disappears seconds before I feel his hand grip the hem of my shirt as he starts to pull upward. I lift my arms but then immediately drop them when I hear the front door open and then slam shut.

I scramble to compose myself, quickly fixing my shirt just seconds before Paxton appears through the half wall that opens up into the living space.

"Hey." Gavin nods toward Paxton before stepping out from between my legs, leaving me sitting on the counter as he resumes collecting the items needed to make our sandwiches.

"Hey." Paxton doesn't seem the least bit surprised to see me here, but I suddenly feel very out of place. "What are you making?" Both men carry on as if Paxton hadn't just walked in on me and Gavin about to have sex directly on top of the kitchen counter.

"Turkey sandwiches," Gavin answers, dropping a loaf of bread on the counter next to me. "You want one?"

"Nah, I'm good." He shakes his head. "I got some shit to take care of. Just needed to stop by and take a quick shower."

"Where've you been?" Gavin questions, laying out two pieces of bread before stacking three slices of turkey on top of each one.

I flip my eyes between the two of them, staying silent as I observe their casual interaction. While Gavin seems completely at ease like he doesn't have a care in the world, Paxton seems kind of anxious.

"I stayed at Dad's last night. We had a few beers with dinner and instead of driving I just decided to crash on his couch."

I don't know why, but I get the feeling something is off with him. Of course, I don't know him well enough to say that as a fact but if I had to guess, there's something going on that he's not letting Gavin in on. I can't help but wonder what it could be. I make a mental note to find out more about Paxton next time I talk to Kimber.

"Nothing. I like it plain," I say when Gavin holds up a bottle of mustard and mayo. He scrunches his nose before slathering his sandwich in mustard.

I'm about to make a comment when the sound of my cell phone signaling a new message from the living room grabs my attention.

"I'll be right back." I slide off the counter.

By the time I reach my purse lying on the couch, Gavin has already moved on to asking Paxton something about his gig at *Deviants* tomorrow night. Honestly, the moment I see the slew of messages that litter my screen, I stop hearing what they are saying.

There has to be at least twenty messages, all from Bryan...

Where are you?
Are you alive?
You missed dinner.
I'm worried. Will you call me, please?

The last one had come in just moments ago. The guilt that previously consumed me comes rushing back like a tidal wave, flooding through every part of my body. I look up to where Gavin and Paxton are still in casual conversation before turning my attention back down to my phone, immediately typing out a quick text.

So sorry. I'm fine. I came to Portland with Kimber last night and my phone died.

I hit send, praying that in his attempt to make sure I was okay that he didn't call Kimber to see if she had heard from me.
His response comes back instantly.

Thank God! I was so worried about you. You missed our date last night.

Shit. Shit. Shit. I totally forgot that we had made dinner plans before I decided to come to Portland to end things with Gavin.

We all know how that turned out for me.

I know. I'm so sorry. I promise I'll make it up to you.

      I hit send, flipping my eyes nervously between my phone and where Gavin is still standing in the kitchen. I feel more than a little guilty for lying to Bryan, but oddly enough I feel even guiltier for texting Bryan while I'm here with Gavin. Fuck me. This situation is so screwed up.

When are you heading back?

      Another incoming message pulls my attention back to my phone.

Not sure. Probably not until tomorrow.

      I immediately pull up Joy's name and shoot her a quick text letting her know I'll have her car home tomorrow. Not that she's missing it. She has four others which is precisely why I don't own one. I can walk almost everywhere and when I need to drive, I know Joy will always let me borrow one of hers. Hell, she'd probably have already bought me three of my own if I would let her.
      Bryan has already text back before I even get the message to Joy sent. When I

finally get to opening his latest message, my stomach knots as the guilt once again smacks me right in the face.

I was hoping to spend some time with you this weekend. Call me as soon as you get home, and I'll come over.

Deal.

I text out one more response before locking my phone, dropping it back into my purse just as Gavin appears in the living room, balancing two plates in one hand and two bottles of water in the other.

"Sorry." I immediately stand, relieving him of one of the plates.

"Everything okay?" he asks, gesturing to where I just put my phone.

"Oh yeah, just fine. I was just texting Joy to let her know I'd have her car back tomorrow," I say, ignoring the little voice in my head chanting *liar*.

"Who says I'm letting you leave at all?" He settles down next to me on the couch before handing me one of the waters.

"Pretty sure you're gonna have to let the girl leave eventually." Paxton appears from the kitchen, a beer clutched in his hand.

"Thank you, Paxton." I nod in his direction before giving Gavin a teasing look.

"Ganged up on by one of my best friends and my girl. Something's wrong with this scenario." He laughs, taking a large bite out of his sandwich despite the fact that his statement has rendered me completely speechless.

My girl... He called me his girl.

The statement causes my heart to pick up speed until it is thudding violently against my ribcage. Paxton quips some smart ass remark at Gavin who only laughs before turning his eyes back to me just as Paxton exits the room.

"You okay?" he asks, clearly seeing something on my face the warrants the question.

"Yeah. I am," I admit truthfully, shaking off my temporary fog. "I'm more than okay." I lean forward, laying a soft kiss to his jaw before turning my attention to my sandwich.

Gavin flips on the television and we eat in silence, both completely enthralled with the latest episode of House Hunters International on HGTV. It's a comfortable silence, one that makes me feel more at ease than I've felt in a very long time.

I find myself flipping my eyes toward Gavin every few minutes, smiling every time I see that adorable grin on his face when he realizes I'm watching him.

When Paxton leaves again less than an

hour later, we are still on the couch, only now we have moved from sitting side by side to me laying with my head in Gavin's lap as his fingers lazily trail through my hair.

Before too long my eyelids start to grow heavy and I find each second more difficult than the last to keep them open. I don't want to sleep. I don't want to miss one moment of this incredible day I've gotten to spend with Gavin. I'm so scared that I will wake up to find it was all some crazy dream.

Unfortunately, that fear is not enough for my body to fight off exhaustion any longer. I don't even realize I've dozed off until I feel Gavin stir beneath me. Seconds later I'm being lifted into the air and cradled against Gavin's chest. I barely register the movement, rolling to the side the moment I feel the mattress beneath me.

Within seconds I feel Gavin's arm snake around me as he settles in behind me. The last thing I remember is his lips grazing the back of my neck and then sleep takes me under once more.

Chapter Thirteen

<u>Harlee</u>

"So why are we here again?" I look at Gavin just seconds after he kills the engine of the truck behind *Deviants*.

"Thought it'd be good to get you out of the condo, show people you're still alive." He winks, pushing open the driver's side door before sliding out.

"By people you mean Kimber." I shake my head, following his actions as I exit the truck, shutting the door behind me.

"I've kept you all to myself for the last two days, and as much as I would love to lock you up and never let you leave, Kimber has requested to see her friend. And by that I mean Decklan has been hounding the shit out of me since Paxton told them you were with me." He laughs, dropping his arm over my shoulder as he leads me toward the rear entrance of the bar.

"I'm not ready to return to the real world just yet," I whine, stopping just feet shy of the door.

A large grin takes over his impossibly handsome face just seconds before he grabs my hand, pulling me to him. Wrapping his arms around me, he drops a kiss to my forehead.

"Neither am I," he admits, holding me just long enough that I know he one hundred percent means his statement.

When he finally releases his hold on me, he spins, pulling open the door before either of us can delay any longer. Waiting for me to enter first, he steps directly in behind me, the sound of Paxton's voice immediately filling my ears. I turn toward the left, catching sight of him sitting in a barstool in the center of the stage, his acoustic guitar resting in his lap as he speaks out to the rather impressive sized crowd for a Sunday night. I don't know why but I expected the place to be a ghost town.

Paxton's wearing tattered jeans partnered with a vintage Smashing Pumpkins shirt, his hair pushed back in its usual style, not a strand out of place. He really does look like a rock star up there. I dare say anyone who witnessed the sight of him would agree with me.

"Come on." Gavin pulls my attention back to him as he wraps his hand around mine and pulls me through the bar.

He leads me toward the back where the majority of the room is made up of high-top round bar tables, not slowing until we reach the back corner where I spot Decklan and Kimber leaning into one another. Their faces are just inches apart, and both have ridiculous smiles pulling up their mouths.

My god they look happy.

I immediately flip my eyes to Gavin, really letting myself grasp for the first time that he has the ability to make me just as happy. When I look at them, I see us in a way. The way Kimber looks at Decklan, the way Decklan looks at Kimber, reminds me a lot of the exchanges Gavin and I have shared over the course of this weekend. The thought makes my stomach twist in both excitement and fear.

Kimber's eyes widen when she spots us approaching, drawing Decklan's attention to our arrival as well. Both sets of eyes follow us until we stop directly next to their table.

"Bout time you two showed up." Decklan leans forward casually, taking a long drink of his beer.

"You're lucky we're here at all," Gavin bites playfully, sliding into the stool next to Decklan which prompts me to take the seat between Gavin and Kimber. "How's he doing?" Gavin gestures toward the stage where Paxton has just begun to play a new song.

I recognize it immediately; *Vulnerable* by Secondhand Serenade. I know it the moment he strums out the first few chords, seeing how it's one of my favorites.

"Really well." Decklan nods, taking another gulp of his beer. "Women are eating him up per usual," he adds.

"No surprise there." Gavin shrugs, turning his attention back to the table.

"Hey girl." Kimber nudges her shoulder against mine, for the first time pulling my gaze to her since we arrived at the table.

Okay so maybe I've been avoiding looking in her direction since I sat down. Clearly, she hasn't missed this fact.

"Hey." I smile, trying to act completely casual.

I don't know why I feel so *weird*.

"You want a drink?" Gavin leans in on my other side, speaking directly into my ear.

"Please." I turn my face inward. "Preferably something with liquor."

He laughs, kissing my temple before pushing into a stand.

"I'll come with you." Decklan immediately stands as well, winking at Kimber before following Gavin toward the bar.

Kimber doesn't even wait until the men are out of earshot before pouncing.

"Spill," she demands, narrowing her eyes on me.

"Spill what?" I try to play it off like this isn't a big deal at all, though deep down I know it's a much bigger deal than even I'm ready to admit.

"How long has this been going on?" She gestures toward the guys who are now standing at the bar.

"It just started. I mean, kind of." I let out a nervous laugh. "I don't even know what *this* is," I admit.

"So you guys are like a thing now?" It's more of a statement than a question, but I choose to answer it like one.

"I guess so." I shrug, not really sure how to label it.

"So I take it you broke things off with Bryan. He must have been heartbroken. You know how much he liked you," she says, her eyes widening when she catches the expression on my face. "No?" She shakes her head.

"I haven't had a chance to. This whole thing happened so fast."

"Harlee, you can't do that. You have to

tell him, like now."

"I know. I just..."

"You just what?" She eyes me curiously.

"What if breaking things off with him isn't the right choice?" I ask hesitantly, fearing the judgment from her I'm sure is soon to come.

I realize how awful of a person this makes me. I'm not stupid enough to believe that my actions here won't have consequences. I'm just not sure I'm ready to face them just yet.

"You can't be serious?" She looks at me like I've got five heads. "From the moment you and Gavin hooked up after Halloween, he's all you talked about."

"Until Bryan," I remind her.

"Even still," she continues like I didn't just interrupt her, "you started dating Bryan because you thought you knew what you were going to get with Gavin. You can't tell me that's still the case. Because if so, then what the hell have you been doing at his condo all weekend?"

"We hooked up that night after dinner. The night you saw us kissing," I admit, knowing in order to make her understand I'm going to have to tell her everything. "I didn't plan for it to happen, nor did I really want it to. It's just when that man touches me; I swear to God, girl, my mind turns to mush."

"Trust me, mush I understand." She reaches out and pats my hand reassuringly.

"So we hooked up and while in the moment it was incredible, I immediately regretted it afterward. I knew how wrong it was, especially because of Bryan. I promised myself right then and there that it wouldn't happen again."

"How is that going for you?" she asks sarcastically, clearly just trying to lighten the situation, which I appreciate.

"Pretty obvious I think." I roll my eyes and let out a frustrated sigh.

"So how did you end up at his place?" She pushes me to continue.

"I went there Friday afternoon to end things. I knew I needed to do it face to face or he would likely just show up, and I didn't want to risk Bryan finding us together. I had every intention of telling him that what happened Thursday night could never happen again, but then he looked at me with those damn blue eyes and crooked smile and it all flew out the window."

"I understand that feeling. I know what it's like to be so completely consumed by a man that you can't see five feet past him. That still doesn't change that what you're doing is wrong," she reminds me.

"I know, he texted me yesterday. Bryan," I add. "I lied. I told him I was spending the weekend in Portland with you." I give her an apologetic look, hating that I dragged her into my lie.

"He never questioned it," I continue. "Not even for a second. Oh God, I really am the worst person in the world." I drop my head into my hands.

"No, you're not. You're human. You just need to make a decision and stick with it. It's not fair for you to drag two men behind you while you decide which one you want to be with."

"I want Gavin," I admit. "But I'm scared. What if he turns out to be exactly the person I thought he was all along and I lose Bryan over it? I don't know what to do."

"Go with your heart." Kimber takes my hand in hers and gives it a light squeeze. "When I questioned my ability to be with Decklan, when I worried that he would hurt me, you were the one who pushed me to conquer that fear. You convinced me that if I felt as deeply for Decklan as I claimed that I would never forgive myself for just giving up and walking away. And you know what? You were right. The only thing I would ever regret would be not fighting for what he and I have." She gives me a small smile.

"Look," she continues. "There are no guarantees in this life. Things might work out, they might not, but can you just walk away without finding out for yourself?"

"I think I'm in love with him," I admit, flipping my eyes to the bar where Decklan and Gavin appear to be in just as deep of a conversation.

"I know you are." She smiles, releasing my hand. "I knew it the moment I saw you two kissing at the restaurant that there was something brewing between you two. My suspicions were confirmed tonight when I saw the way he was looking at you. I'd say you're not alone in those feelings."

"Really?" I don't know why her statement surprises me but it does.

"I've been around Gavin long enough to know he doesn't really do the girlfriend thing. You are the only girl I've ever seen him come into the bar with. Usually, he just leaves with them and even then it's always random girls that I never see again. It's different this time. I can see it. It's not just Bryan's heart on the line anymore."

"What do I do?" I ask, ignoring the jealousy that creeps in at the mention of Gavin with other women.

"I can't tell you that. What I can tell you is that the longer you wait to break things off with Bryan, or Gavin— whichever you choose— the harder and messier it's going to be. My advice: make a choice now and stick with it."

I open my mouth to say more but then close it again when Kimber gestures behind me. I turn just in time to see Gavin slide in next to me, a bright pink drink garnished with pineapple and a cherry in one hand, his usual beer in the other.

"Sex on the Beach." He sets the drink in front of me before reclaiming his seat.

I immediately take a long drink, the cold, fruity liquid mildly soothing the uneasiness that has settled in my chest.

"Good?" He smiles, gesturing to the drink.

"Amazing," I admit, taking another long sip.

"Val makes the best mixed drinks," Decklan interjects, pulling my attention to where he has slid in next to Kimber and now has her small frame tucked against him.

"I think I have to agree," I admit, taking another drink.

I honestly don't know if the drink is really that good or if I'm just so desperate to numb the storm brewing inside of me that I'm not even really registering what it tastes like. Either way, I can tell almost immediately that it's doing the trick.

Slowly— over the course of the next few minutes— I feel the warmth start to spread across my face, the amount of liquor in the drink clearly more than I originally thought. I relish in the feeling, loving how little by little my fear and uneasiness start to fall into the background, and I find myself rather enjoying the casual conversation that floats among the four of us.

Watching Decklan and Gavin is like watching an old married couple. They bicker back and forth, disagree about everything, and never seem to see eye to eye, but the bond between them is undeniable.

By my second drink I am an active participant at the table, retelling the story of how when we were seventeen, Angel and I were forced to walk two miles home completely naked. It was late one summer night after her brother's friend had stolen our clothes when we decided to take them off and jump into the local swimming pond.

First and last time I've ever been skinny dipping. Having to walk two miles in the middle of the night, ducking behind trees to avoid being seen was enough to teach me my lesson there. My feet hurt for days afterward considering along with no clothes, I also had no shoes.

I swear I think Kimber laughed harder than I've ever seen her laugh before. Probably because she knows me and Angel both very well and picturing this little adventure is not that hard for her to do.

The guys spend the next hour retelling

their own stories from childhood. Decklan jumping an old dirt bike over two derby cars and nearly breaking his neck. Gavin getting so high that he spent two hours laying in the grass, watching the stars as he sung himself lullabies.

Drink after drink, hour after hour, time just seems to slip away. I'm completely captivated by Gavin; watching him speak, watching his reaction when Decklan tells us something funny from their past.

I swear I fall harder and harder with each second that ticks by until I can no longer even remember why I was hesitant to begin with. His eyes, his smile, the way he looks at me when he catches me staring; I swear I could spend the rest of my life just staring at this beautiful man.

We end up staying at the bar well past close. Paxton joins us after his last set and the stories continue well into the early morning hours. By the time Gavin finally leads me to the truck, the sun has already started to peek out over the horizon.

Stopping just feet from his truck, I look over to find him watching me curiously.

"What?" I ask, suddenly self-conscious.

"You're fucking beautiful, you know that?" His crooked smile is enough to send my heart galloping inside my chest.

"I'm also very hungry." I crinkle my

nose, reaching for his hand.

The second his fingers close around mine, I tug, pulling him toward me.

"What's a girl gotta do to get some pancakes around here?" I tease, pushing up to lay a gentle kiss to his mouth before pulling back.

"I can think of a few things," he teases, tightening his grip on me.

"After pancakes." I kiss him again, loving how at ease I suddenly feel with him.

"Fine. After pancakes." He smiles, laying his lips to mine once more.

Chapter Fourteen

Harlee

Returning to my dorm room after spending the weekend with Gavin feels more like entering an alternate universe rather than stepping back into my normal life. I spend most of the afternoon cat napping, considering I never actually went to bed Sunday night.

By five o'clock, I am up and as determined as ever to set this whole mess straight once and for all. Kimber's right. I need to make a decision and stick with it.

Holding my cell phone in my hand, I stare at it for a long moment before finally pressing Bryan's number. I feel like my heart is beating out of my chest as it rings; once, twice, his voice finally sounding on the line before it can ring a third time.

"Hey." I can hear the usual smile in his voice.

"Hey."

"How was Portland?" he asks.

"It was fun. I enjoyed myself." Guilt floods through me all over again.

"Good. I'm glad. But I missed the hell out of you."

"I missed you, too."

I wish I could say my statement is the truth, but honestly, I thought very little about him for most of the weekend. I was too caught up in Gavin to really see anything past that incredible smile of his.

"Do you think you can come over?" I ask, silently praying that he says no.

I know I need to get this over with, but I really don't know how I'm going to. Just talking to him reminds me what an amazing guy he is. When I close my eyes I can see his messy hair and laid back smile.

He has this incredible way of making me feel so comfortable, no matter what's going on around us. He makes me laugh. He's dependable. He gets along with everyone. And most importantly, he doesn't play games, which is more than I can say for Gavin.

My heart knows what it wants... Gavin.

But my head is still battling back and forth between the sensible, smart choice and the choice that lights my soul on fire.

"Oh, babe. I wish I could." Bryan's voice pulls me from my inner battle and back to the present conversation. "I have my Ethics class in ten minutes. Monday night remember?" he reminds me.

"Oh, that's right. I forgot you have two evening classes this semester."

"How about dinner tomorrow night?" he suggests.

"Yeah okay, that sounds good," I agree, for the first time realizing that meeting him in public might be easier.

At least that way he will be less likely to cause a scene when I drop the bomb on him that I've fallen in love with another man. Oh God, he has no idea this is even coming and here I'm just going to walk in there and crush him.

Panic tightens my chest, making it almost impossible to suck in a good breath.

"Harlee, did you hear me?" Bryan's voice washes over me.

"What?" The word comes out breathless.

"Are you okay?" He seems genuinely concerned which only adds to the guilt.

"I'm fine. Sorry, I didn't get much sleep this weekend." I try to reel myself back in.

"Well get some rest," he instructs. "I

gotta get into class. I'll pick you up tomorrow, six o'clock?"

"Actually, just text me the location and I'll meet you there. I have one of Joy's cars that I need to return to her. I can just drop it off after dinner."

"Sounds good. Talk to you soon."

"Okay."

"I love you." His words catch me off guard, momentarily paralyzing my ability to respond.

Without another word he ends the call, clearly chalking up my silence as I've already hung up. I drop the phone into my lap, taking several deep breaths trying to calm the rush of emotion that has suddenly washed over me.

He said he loves me...

This situation just got a whole hell of a lot more complicated.

****

Getting through the day of classes was damn near unbearable. Not even Angel's witty remarks and sexual comments about our English professor could pull me from the foul mood I woke up in.

The only highlight of my entire day was a text message I got from Gavin just as I was getting ready for my dinner date with Bryan.

I can still smell you in my bed.
I fucking love it.

It shouldn't have brought a smile to my face, knowing what was to come, but it did. It made me wish I was there with him, lost in our own little world. Suddenly I didn't know if I was more upset over what I was about to do to Bryan, or about the fact that all I wanted to do was be with Gavin and couldn't be. At least not until Thursday after classes.

God, since when does two days seem like an eternity of time?

I drop Joy's Mercedes off with the valet at *Truman's Fish Market*, an upscale restaurant known for its fresh seafood selection, just fifteen minutes from campus. I've been here a couple times with Joy, but it's been a while. Regardless I doubt it's suddenly become a restaurant where you can secure a reservation one day in advance, which means Bryan has had this planned for at least a few days. This knowledge makes me even more nervous.

Handing my jacket to the younger man working the coat check, I immediately smooth the knee-length black cocktail dress I chose for tonight, wishing I had settled on a material less likely to wrinkle so easily.

"Harlee." I hear Bryan's voice just moments before he is standing directly in front of me.

He's wearing black pants and a dark gray button-down; much more formal than the normal casual beach bum attire he usually sports. His hair is combed back and when I finally meet his gaze, he's wearing a ridiculously excited look.

"Hey." I plaster on my best smile, not pulling away when he leans in for a soft kiss.

While it doesn't light the same fire as Gavin's kiss, it still causes a mild simmer beneath my skin. Truth is if I felt nothing for Bryan this would be much easier. Unfortunately, I have really grown to care for him over the past couple of months.

"You look beautiful." He pulls back, his smile still firmly in place.

"And you—" I gesture to his outfit, "—very handsome."

"I didn't think a place like this would appreciate my board shorts," he laughs. "Come on. Our table is ready, but I wanted to wait for you at the door." He gently guides me into the restaurant, his hand placed firmly against the small of my back.

'What's this all about?" I ask, taking a seat in the chair he pulls out for me. "This place is much fancier than our normal dinner dates."

"Well, today is not just any other date." He takes a seat across the small two person table from me. "Today we are celebrating."

"And what exactly are we celebrating?" I ask, pausing when the waiter arrives to take our drink order.

Bryan waits until the redheaded twenty-something disappears before continuing.

"Do you know what today is?" he asks, raising his eyebrows up and down at me.

I think for a long moment but can't come up with anything.

"Should I?" I ask, apology lining my face.

"Probably not," he laughs. "I'm sure I'm the only man on the planet who celebrates a two month anniversary."

"What?" The word falls from my mouth.

His statement catches me off guard, the pure adoration written all over his face more than a little overwhelming.

"Two months ago today, you officially became my girlfriend. It took me weeks to get you to finally agree to even go on a date with me, but once you did... Well, that was one of the happiest days of my life. I knew there was no way I was going to let you slip through my fingers." He reaches across the table, twisting his hand around mine. "Which is why I am starting our first tradition. Every two months, on this date, I propose we do something special together. Something that reminds us how we felt then and how those feelings have grown into so much more since."

"I don't know what to say," I blurt, emotion clogging my throat.

Here I expected some easy dinner where I would gently break things off with him. Now I have no idea what the hell to do. How do you break up with someone who clearly put so much into making this date special?

"You don't have to say anything. I don't need anything from you, Harlee. No words. No actions. I just need you." He squeezes my hand, not breaking away until the waiter returns with our drinks.

Thankful to have a moment to compose my thoughts, I nod to the waiter before quickly skimming the menu.

"Would you like a few moments?" he asks, gesturing to the menu.

"No, I know what I want. Do you know what you want?" I nervously ramble.

"Go ahead." Bryan laughs lightly, clearly not reading anything into my reaction.

Within two minutes our orders are placed and once again the waiter disappears, leaving me in the corner with this sweet, incredible man who's heart I came here to break.

Only now I don't think I can do it.

Maybe that's selfish of me, but right now I don't care. I can't just end things with him like this. He deserves better. He deserves so much more than the less than stellar girlfriend I've been. The least I can do is give him tonight. One more night...

I swallow down my original plan and do my best to pretend like this is any other night and the events that have taken place over this past week never happened at all. Surprisingly it's easier than I thought it would be.

Our conversation flows seamlessly throughout our meal. We talk, we laugh, and we hold hands. It's all so natural. It isn't until we exit the restaurant nearly two hours later that the reality of my situation starts to creep back in.

The little voice in my head returns. The one that taunts me, calling me a whore and a liar. It's more prominent now than ever before and maybe that's because what I am doing right now is unforgivable.

I'm giving Bryan false hope. I'm making him believe that our future stretches beyond tonight when in all reality this is the last date we will ever have.

It's bittersweet.

On one hand, I feel horrible and even a little heartbroken over the thought of me and Bryan never existing like this again. On the other, I know that Gavin is waiting for me on the other side.

I made my choice. Now I just have to see it through.

Bryan holds my hand and waits next to me until the valet finally pulls around with Joy's car. Turning toward me, he gazes deeply into my eyes. I feel like he's searching for something but I can't quite figure out what.

"Harlee..." he pauses, nervously biting his bottom lip, "...when I said I loved you last night, I meant it," he admits, seeming uncharacteristically backward.

"Bryan... I," I start.

"Don't. You don't have to say anything. I just wanted to tell you in person so you know it's real. I love you," he says, leaning in to lay a sweet kiss to my mouth.

Once again I can feel the thick emotion clog my throat, and I fight back the welling tears as I tighten my grip on him, deepening the kiss. I know I'm doing it for my benefit; my way of saying goodbye, and I'm so ashamed of the action. But in this moment, I don't care. I just want him to know that no matter what happens from here on out, my feelings for him were always real.

I truly care for Bryan. I would even go as far as to say that I love him. Maybe not in the way I love Gavin, but in a way that you love someone that over time becomes a part of who you are as a whole.

I finally break the kiss, laying my forehead against his.

"Goodnight, Bryan," I get out

breathlessly, turning around and quickly climbing into the Mercedes without looking in his direction again.

I'm not even out of the parking lot before the tears start to fall. I'm so pissed at myself. I'm pissed that I couldn't do what I came here to do. I'm pissed that I put myself in a position to have to do it in the first place.

I know I need to take Joy's car back, but right now there is one place I know I need to be. A place where I know I get no judgments. A place that feels more like home than any other place on this earth.

I grab my cell and pull up Angel's number. She answers on the first ring.

"I'm coming over," I croak, not wasting time with pleasantries.

"I'll have the tequila ready." She reads me immediately, ending the call without another word.

One great thing about having a friend like Angel is knowing that no matter what I need, she'll always be there. It's the type of friendship where sentences are finished and when one needs the other, everything else ceases to exist.

I need a shoulder, some tequila shots, and maybe even a good punch in the face for how fucking stupid I am for getting so mixed up in all of this.

I hit the gas pedal, loving the way the

engine purrs under my sudden acceleration. I just need to get to Angel's and forget this night ever happened. There will plenty of time to beat myself up tomorrow. Tonight I just need to exist without Bryan or Gavin. I need to exist in a world where I'm not the girl torn between two men but just Harlee.

Within ten minutes, I am headed down the long, paved driveway that leads back to Angel's parents house which sits about a quarter of a mile off the roadway. Parking the car around back, I head straight for the small gray-sided guest house that sits several feet behind the main house.

Angel moved out of the main house after we graduated high school. I still remember how it took her weeks to convince her parents to let her move out here. She insisted that living in the guest house would give her a semblance of freedom while still remaining safely at home. I think her mom was sold from the beginning. It was her dad she really had to convince.

The front door swings open before I even reach the landing, and Angel appears in the doorway. Her shoulder length black hair is pinned back away from her face and she's wearing the ugliest pink pajamas I've ever seen. She's owned them for as long as I can remember and I swear as often as she wears them, it's a wonder they are still in one piece.

She gets one good look at me as I approach and immediately opens her arms, wrapping them around me the moment I reach her.

"You look like shit." She squeezes me tightly before releasing me.

"You're one to talk," I bite playfully, pushing past her into the house.

I cross the small space to the corner where a fluffy gray couch is pressed against the far wall. Collapsing on top of it, I let out a frustrated groan, rubbing my hand across my forehead.

"That bad huh?" She appears next to me, flopping down to my right.

"Worse." I turn my face toward her, just now noticing the bottle of tequila in her hand.

"Wanna talk about it?" She smiles, dangling it in front of me.

Snagging the bottle from her hand, I quickly cross to the opposite wall that houses a small, galley style kitchen. Pulling down two shot glasses from the cabinet like I have so many times before, I set them on the counter before filling each one to the rim.

"First, we drink." I hand Angel her shot when she comes to stand next to me in the kitchen.

We clink glasses and drink our shots in unison.

Only a friend like Angel would let me

show up at her house this late on a weeknight with no explanation and immediately start drinking with me. No matter what else happens, at least I have her.

My friends are something I will never take for granted. At the end of the day, when all of this is said and done, they may be all I have left.

Chapter Fifteen

<u>Gavin</u>

"Oh shit, this has trouble written all over it," Decklan says, exiting his apartment to find me and Paxton lounging at the bar, a bottle of scotch sitting directly between us.

"Where's your old lady?" Paxton leans forward to refill his glass.

"Asleep." He flips his eyes between the two of us. "Like you fuckers should probably be," he says, sliding out the stool next to Paxton before taking a seat.

"Because you're fucking one to talk." I lean forward, grabbing a rocks glass from the other side of the counter before sliding it down the bar toward Deck. "Now shut the fuck up and have a drink with us," I say.

"Didn't you hear?" Paxton interjects. "Deck here is too good to hang out with us now."

"Fuck you," Decklan huffs, snagging the bottle of scotch off the bar before filling his glass.

"No really, it's cool," Paxton continues. "Trade your brothers in for a chick. We see how it is."

"What can I say; she smells better than you fuckers and is much better to look at, too." He gives Paxton an evil grin before swigging down the contents of his glass.

"I'm hurt. Are you saying we're not pretty enough for you?" I chime in.

I love getting the opportunity to bust Decklan's balls. I get to do it so little these days.

"That's exactly what I'm saying." He laughs, refilling his glass. "Seriously, though, what the fuck are you guys still doing here?" His question prompts me to look up at the clock for the first time in a while.

"Fuck, is it really four in the morning?" I turn wide eyes on Paxton who just shrugs before taking another drink of his scotch.

"We were just bullshitting," I finally answer his original question. "Why aren't you in bed yourself?"

"Couldn't sleep." He takes another long

drink.

I know immediately that he must have had another nightmare. He's had them for years, since the car accident he was in when he was seventeen. His fourteen-year-old brother Conner died in that accident and it has haunted him ever since. I remember right after the accident, they were so bad he would wake up screaming bloody murder in the middle of the night. Scared the shit out of me the first couple times it happened.

"Thought you said they were better?" I ask, not bothering to ask why he can't sleep given that I already know.

"They are," he agrees, "but every now and again one will hit me pretty hard. It's shifted a bit, though. Now instead of seeing Conner's face, I see Kimber's. Fucks with me every fucking time. I'm like some crazy fucking parent waking up to make sure my baby is still breathing." He shakes his head, taking another long drink.

"I think I know what might help you get some sleep." Paxton's eyes light up as he reaches into the front pocket of his casual button-down shirt, moments later pulling out a joint.

"Where the fuck did you get that?" I throw my head back on a laugh.

I haven't smoked pot since I was probably nineteen or twenty. I don't know why, just kind of outgrew it I guess.

"Matt gave it to me," he says, referring to one of our part-time bartenders.

"Figures." Deck shakes his head, reaching for the joint. "Matt would be the one to be giving away drugs in our bar." He holds it up in front of his face and inspects it for a long moment. "Guess we shouldn't let it go to waste." He looks down the bar to me.

"Light the shit up," I say, seeing no reason not to. "Fuck it."

"And here I thought you fuckers had gone soft on me," Paxton quips.

He throws his head back on a laugh when Deck lights the joint and takes a deep inhale, his eyes widening as he tries to hold it in without coughing. Finally after several long moments, he lets out a stream of thick smoke, the smell of weed instantly filling the space.

"Fuck. I forgot how good that shit tastes," he says, passing the joint to Paxton who hits it like a pro before handing it to me.

"Oh shit," I mutter, looking at the joint in my hand wondering what in the hell I just got myself into.

"Don't be a fucking pussy. Hit it already." Paxton shoves at my shoulder.

"I got this," I reassure him, lifting the joint to my lips.

I take a deep inhale, trying my damnedest not to cough as I struggle to hold the smoke in my lungs. I finally blow it out slowly, feeling the familiar buzz already starting to creep its way in.

We continue to pass the joint around until there is nothing left but a little roach too small to even hold between our fingers, by which point I'm beyond just being high. I feel like I just smoked myself stupid.

My surroundings seem to shift and everything slows down around me. I look over at Decklan and immediately bust out in laughter. His eyes are completely bloodshot, and he's squinting like he's having trouble keeping them open.

"Holy shit." He starts laughing, too. "I'm fucking stoned."

This is all it takes for Paxton too, and the next thing I know we are all laughing like a bunch of teenagers.

We spend the next hour reminiscing on all the times we used to sneak out into the woods behind Paxton's dad's house and smoke, and all the crazy shit we used to do after getting high.

Over time the laughter falls away, and I find myself in the middle of maybe one of the most intense conversations I've shared with Paxton and Decklan in a very long time.

I listen to Paxton talk about his mom, how hard it was to watch her slip away little by little, the cancer killing her from the inside out. I listen to Deck talk about how terrified he is that he's going to fuck things up with Kimber, and how he finally finds himself wanting a family of his own. It's the first time I've ever heard him mention kids, but I don't miss the way his face lights up as he talks about the possibility of being a father.

I have felt a distance between all three of us for a long time now and it feels so good to just sit together and hash out all our shit. Sometimes you just need to fucking say shit out loud to get it the fuck off your chest.

When the conversation starts to taper off, I take a deep breath and finally say my own piece.

"I think I'm in love." Harlee's face flashes through my mind the way it seems to do a hundred times per day.

"Tell us something we don't already know." Paxton turns toward me, his mouth turned up in a wide smile.

"Wait, what?" I retort.

"Dude, you're about as obvious as they come," He continues, Deck nodding in agreement behind him. "I knew almost instantly that this was gonna be the girl." He pauses. "The girl who finally woke you the fuck up," he clarifies.

"How could you possibly know that when I'm just realizing it myself?" I hate that apparently, I'm that fucking transparent.

"You're so caught up in Harlee, dude; I'm surprised you can see what's happening right in front of you," Decklan chimes in.

"Cause you're one to talk," I counter.

"He *can't* see what's happening," Paxton says to Decklan, agreeing with his prior statement before turning toward me. "For fucks sake, you're balls deep over this girl and she still has a fucking boyfriend."

"Not after this past weekend, she doesn't." I finish off the last of my scotch in one drink.

"She ended things with him?" Decklan seems surprised by this news.

"I mean, she hasn't said as much but yeah, as far as I can tell they're done. I don't need her to confirm that she's told him. She said she wanted to be with me. I'm gonna take that as she's made her choice."

"Okay then." Paxton shakes his head in disagreement.

"What the fuck is it?" I question, not liking his reaction.

"All I'm saying is you better get that shit in writing. Lock it down that you're exclusive at least. For all you know she could be playing you both. Some women like to see how far they can push a man before he finally reaches his breaking point." He refills his glass and takes a long gulp.

"Why do I get the feeling we aren't

talking about Harlee anymore?" I eye him curiously.

Something is up with him. I can't believe I just now noticed, but it's blaringly clear.

"I'm just saying." He shrugs like it's nothing.

"Fuck that." I shake my head. "What the fuck is going on with you?"

"Nothing," he insists. "Really it's nothing." He looks between me and Deck.

I open my mouth to push for more but refrain when I hear a throat clear, snapping me from the fog I feel like I've been in for the last couple of hours. Looking toward the door that leads up to Decklan's apartment, we all freeze when we realize Kimber is standing in the doorway, her arms crossed in front of her chest, her pretty face turned up in a playful scowl.

"Seriously guys?" She steps toward the bar, letting the door swing closed behind her. "This place smells like a fraternity house." She crinkles her nose.

"That's my fault." Paxton immediately takes the heat.

"I'm not your mother." A smile spreads across her face as she steps up to the counter on the opposite side of us, immediately reaching for the scotch. "Drinking the good stuff tonight I see." She sets the bottle down and turns her eyes to Decklan. "You okay?"

She mouths even though we are all looking at her to see what she's saying.

I flip my eyes to Deck who nods yes and reaches for her hand which she willingly extends to him.

"We didn't wake you did we?" he asks, closing his fingers around hers.

"No. I'm used to sleeping through the noise. You three have nothing on a packed bar." She leans forward, resting her elbows on the bar directly across from Decklan. "So what are we talking about?" She eyes the three of us curiously.

"Gavin's in love," Paxton blurts, throwing the attention my way.

"What the fuck, dude," I object. "What the fuck happened to keeping shit in the circle?" I ask, referring to the fact that what we say to each other stays with us and only us.

"Duh," Kimber's response pulls my attention back to her. "Don't look at me like that. You're so obvious it's almost a little pathetic." She grins playfully. "But if it makes you feel any better, I think the only person more clueless than you is Harlee." Her smile widens.

"Well thank fuck for that." I sigh, pinching the bridge of my nose between my fingers as I feel the effects of a small headache working its way in.

"Come on, I'll drive you two home,"

Kimber offers, releasing Decklan's hand.

"You don't have to do that," he immediately interjects.

"Considering they've been here drinking all night, yes, yes I do," she insists. "I can take Gavin's truck. I'll drop them off and then bring the truck back here until later."

"I'll just follow you over and bring you back on my bike." The moment the words leave Decklan's mouth, Kimber cocks her head to the side and narrows her eyes at him.

"Nope, you're right. I'm going to go upstairs and try to sleep it off," he says without her having to say another word.

"Now that's what you call balls deep," I tease the moment he slides out of the bar stool.

"Yeah. Yeah. Fuck you. I know I'm whipped," he says, stepping directly in front of Kimber. "And I wouldn't have it any fucking other way." He plants a deep kiss on her lips.

I immediately look away, as does Paxton, suddenly feeling like I'm intruding on a very private moment. I've seen Deck make out with countless girls, but there's something very different about seeing him kiss a woman he loves. It's more intimate and private. For the first time in my life, I'm actually able to relate. The thought makes me miss Harlee even more than I already do.

"You can look now." Kimber pulls my

attention back to where she's standing, a wide smile plastered across her face. "You, bed." She opens the door leading upstairs and ushers Decklan through it, pushing the door shut behind him. "You two, come on." She gestures toward the back entrance.

"Fuck. Now I really feel like a fucking teenager again," I whine, pushing off my stool.

"But Mom, I'm not ready to leave yet," Paxton continues the joke, calling after her as she pushes open the back door.

Sunshine filters into the bar and for the first time, I realize that it's daylight outside. Fuck... Where did the time go?

"Don't make me tell you twice." She purposely tries to make her voice sound more parental, pulling the back door shut as soon as we're all outside.

I squint into the bright sun, following Kimber as she leads the way toward my truck that's parked toward the back of the lot.

"You know, you don't have to drive us home. I can call a cab," I object when she holds her palm out for my keys.
"I realize this, but it's a five-minute drive and there's no sense in paying an arm and a leg for a cab when I can just take you really quick." She nods when I drop the keys in her hand.

"Now get in," she orders, waiting until both Paxton and I are in the cab of the truck before climbing in.

"You realize you're still in your pajamas right?" I ask, just now noticing that she's wearing one of Decklan's old t-shirts, a pair of ratty looking plaid pajama bottoms, and thick pink house shoes. She didn't even bother to put on a jacket despite the fact that it's freezing this morning.

"And?" She gives me a look that says she couldn't care less before sticking the key in the ignition and firing the truck to life.

"Girls." Paxton looks at Kimber and then back to me before shrugging.

"I'm sorry. Would you rather I go get dressed before driving your two drunk asses home?" she nips playfully.

"Sorry, Mom," Paxton jokes, shrinking down in the seat.

"Boys." She sighs, shaking her head as she pulls the truck out of the parking lot and heads in the direction of my condo.

Chapter Sixteen

<u>Harlee</u>

I look up from the textbook laying in my lap when a loud knock sounds against the door to my dorm room. Looking at the clock on my bedside table, I see it's just after eight in the evening. Not sure who it could be, I drop the book next to me on the bed and push into a stand, quickly reaching the door just as another knock echoes through the room.

Sliding the lock, I crack the door open just enough so that I can see into the hallway, letting it fall the rest of the way open the moment his blue eyes find mine.

"What are you—" I start to ask but before I can finish my sentence, Gavin quickly steps forward, his mouth immediately closing down on mine.

The contact instantly silences my attempt to speak as he backs me into my dorm room and kicks the door closed behind him.

"God, I fucking missed you," he growls against my lips, deepening the kiss as his hands immediately go for the band of my yoga pants.

His fingers slide inside the elastic waist moments before he rips them and my panties down in one quick tug.

As much as him showing up unannounced is a surprise to me, it takes my body no time at all to adjust to his presence. Within seconds I can feel the familiar buzz start to work its way through my limbs, the fire of his touch sending heat spiraling through my entire body.

"I just couldn't wait any longer." He breaks away from my mouth just long enough to pull my hooded sweatshirt over my head and toss it to the floor.

"Fuck me," he rasps as his eyes trace down my chest, taking in my bare torso. "You're so fucking beautiful." His lips dip to my neck, his tongue flicking across the base of my throat.

I let my head fall back, my hands tangling in his hair as I anchor my arms around his neck.

"I can't wait another second to be inside you." His mouth finds mine again as he backs me toward the bed.

The moment the mattress hits the back of my knees, I collapse on top of it, Gavin coming down directly on top of me. Kicking my pants the rest of the way off, I wrap my legs around his waist, moaning when he grinds his erection into me through the material of his jeans.

I pull at his shirt, sliding it over his head when he pulls back slightly to make the task easier for me. My fingers trace the defined muscles of his chest, sliding lower along his abs as he hovers above me, his arms holding up the brunt of his weight.

I flip my hand up, palming his erection which causes him to close his eyes as he grinds into my touch. The look of pure *lust* in his eyes when they finally open again sends a whole other wave of desire coursing through me.

I unbutton his pants, ripping open the zipper before helping slide them off his hips. The moment his erection springs free, I wrap my hand around it, sliding it from the base to the tip. He groans again, this time, his eyes not leaving mine.

Lining him up at my entrance, he pauses, looking down at me curiously.

"It's okay, you can do it," I reassure him, letting him know that I'm protected and that I trust him.

His eyes burn even wilder when the realization finally sinks in and he immediately thrust forward, filling me so full so quickly that I can't help but cry out from the sudden overwhelming feeling that spurs through me.

"Oh fuck," he breathes, dropping his face into my neck as he pulls out and thrusts back in. "Fuck, baby, you feel so fucking good." He stills for a moment to really allow himself to feel me bare around him.

"So fucking good," he repeats, his mouth finding mine as he slowly starts moving in and out of me.

I didn't realize how much different it would feel having him inside of me like this, with no barrier between us. There are no words to describe how incredible it is to feel every inch of him pumping inside of me, seeing the pleasure my body is giving him when he pulls back and meets my gaze.

That's when it hits me, the first wave. It builds and builds making me feel like my body might split apart at any moment. I close my eyes but Gavin forces them back open, taking me by the chin.

"Eyes on me. I want to watch you." He thrusts harder, his words and movements splitting the last thread holding me together in two.

I fall apart beneath him, struggling not

to turn away from his gaze as the pleasure crashes through me over and over again. I can see his control faltering almost instantly. A wildness takes over his gaze as he pounds into me relentlessly, his gaze still firmly holding mine.

I'm still riding out the last remaining pleasure of my orgasm when he finds his release as well, spilling himself inside me. A different kind of pleasure takes hold of me and I rock my hips, meeting him thrust for thrust until he finally collapses down on top of me. His lips immediately go to my neck, trailing soft kisses across my flesh as we both work to catch our breath and compose ourselves.

"Holy fuck." I can feel his smile against my skin.

"Yeah," I agree, the word just a whisper.

"Holy fuck," he repeats, happiness evident in his voice. "That was..." He pulls back to look at me, his face hovering just inches above mine. "Fuck." He shakes his head slightly. "You're fucking incredible." He smiles, dropping his mouth to mine.

He kisses me deeply for several long moments, his softening erection coming to life again still buried deep inside me. He moves slightly, testing to see my reaction to his eagerness to go again.

Fortunately for him, I was ready to go again before the first time was even over.

Smiling against his mouth, I raise my hips, egging him forward. It doesn't take long before he's moving in and out of me, his pace slow and steady while his lips remain on mine.

The first time was all about satisfying the hunger building inside of both of us, having been nearly a week since we've seen each other. But this time, this is something so much more intense on a completely different level.

He slides his tongue against mine, rolling his hips as my fingers tangle into his hair. My entire body feels like a wind-up toy. He keeps spinning my dial over and over, just waiting for the moment when he can release me and watch me roll straight over the edge.

"Harlee." His word is just a whisper against my lips as I feel his body once again start to go rigid around me. His muscles clench and tighten as he continues his slow, controlled movements.

"Do it," I urge him forward, my body already hanging on the edge for the past several minutes.

That's all it takes and in one deep groan into my mouth he lets go of his release, my orgasm following directly behind. I wrap my arms around his neck and hold on for dear life, our teeth clattering together as we swallow up the cries of pleasure blending between the two of us.

It's the most intense and overwhelming orgasm I've ever had, and I know one hundred percent that it has everything to do with the fact that it's no longer just sex with Gavin. There's a deeper meaning, a need to claim not only each other's bodies but each other's hearts as well.

When Gavin relaxes down on me this time, there are no words said. In fact, neither of us seems to be in any hurry to do anything but enjoy the aftermath of what we just shared. We are beyond words now. My body has already told him everything he needs to know.

I am his... As if there was ever any question to begin with.

****

"I'm so happy you're here." I snuggle against Gavin's chest, still not believing this is real.

The whole situation feels more like a fantasy than anything that could actually happen, especially to me. I'm simply not this lucky. And yet, here he is; laying in my bed, warm beneath my touch. I'm so lost in this man, it's hard for me to determine where I end and he begins.

"Me too." He lays a kiss on the top of my head, tightening his grip on me. "I'm sorry to show up without calling, but not seeing you wasn't a fucking option." He laughs lightly, the sound vibrating beneath my cheek.

"I would expect no less." I smile, finally coming to terms with the fact that this man is going to do what he wants when he wants and be damned if anyone is going to tell him otherwise.

It's one of the things I have come to love about him the most. His fearlessness. His drive. His unwavering determination.

"So I have a confession." He shifts slightly so he can look down at my face. "I also came here to ask you something." He tilts my chin up before laying a light kiss to my mouth. "I was hoping you would join me for lunch tomorrow at my mom's house." His words instantly send my heart galloping against my ribcage. "I thought you'd have a harder time saying no to me in person." He rubs his nose against mine.

"What?" I pull back slightly, not able to hide my surprise.

Are we at that point already? He's ready for me to meet his mom? I'm not sure if I should be excited or scared shitless, but I'm suddenly feeling a little bit of both.

"I know it seems like a big step but it's completely casual, I swear. Decklan and Kimber are going. Paxton will probably stop by. I doubt any of my other family will be there with the exception of maybe Charlie, and even then I'm not sure about her."

"I..." I start but he cuts me off before I can get more than the one word out.

"I thought it would be a nice way to kind of ease you in. To be honest, my family can be a bit nuts, and the last thing I want to do is overwhelm you," he rambles.

It isn't until this exact moment that I see how nervous he is. It seems odd, watching a man like Gavin clearly struggle to do something as simple as inviting me to his mom's house for lunch. This knowledge instantly calms any reservations I may have had about it.

"I'd love to," I cut him off just as he opens his mouth to say more.

"Yeah?" He smiles down at me, a wide boyish grin that causes my breath to catch in my throat.

"Yes," I say, pushing up to kiss his jaw.

"So I have to ask you something else." He tucks me back against his chest, his tone falling more serious. "You and Bryan, it's over right?" His question causes my chest to constrict in panic, and I blurt my answer before really thinking it through.

"Yes."

I try to hide the sudden tremble that runs through me at the lie. I mean, it's not entirely untrue. In my mind, Bryan and I are over. Now whether or not he knows it is a different story entirely.

I haven't had the opportunity to talk to him since our dinner two nights ago and as horrible as I feel for not just doing it then, I feel even worse now spewing my lies to Gavin. What the fuck is wrong with me? I'm normally a very straightforward, honest person, but this situation has turned me into a person I can barely stand to look at in the mirror.

I don't know where my hesitation is stemming from. I want Gavin. I know I want Gavin. I just can't seem to bring myself to utter those words to Bryan.

Is it because I'm afraid of hurting him? Because a part of me isn't ready to let him go? Because I'm still unsure about Gavin's true intentions? I'm not really sure at this point. Maybe it's a little bit of all of them.

Gavin accepts my answer without question, shifting me to my side so he can tuck in behind me. He drops his face into my hair, pulling my back as close to his chest as he can get it. He lets out a deep sigh, relaxing into the mattress.

I lay there for what feels like an eternity, staring out into the darkness of the room; my mind swirls with the truth of my lies. I don't know at what point Gavin slipped off to sleep, only that his breathing eventually slowed and evened.

I listen to each intake of air, counting the seconds between each breath as he sleeps peacefully behind me. The reality of how much I love this man is staggering. Even listening to him breath makes my heartbeat quicken.

I have to tell Bryan. I have to tell him as soon as possible. I can't risk jeopardizing Gavin's trust. I won't. As much as I don't want to hurt Bryan, the thought of hurting Gavin is even more crippling.

I won't do it over the phone; he deserves more than that. But I will do it, and soon. No one tells you how hard these things are. I've never been in a situation to care enough about hurting someone, let alone two someones. This has to end, and I'm the only one that can make that happen.

It's about time I prove to myself that there's nothing I won't endure to be with Gavin. Because at the end of the day, he is the only thing in this world I know with complete certainty I don't want to live without.

Chapter Seventeen

Harlee

"I'm so glad you came." Kimber smiles from ear to ear, pulling me into a tight hug just moments after I step inside Gavin's mom's house.

"Hey," I say, pulling back to meet her gaze the moment she releases me.

"When Gavin said he was inviting you, I thought there was no way you would agree." She loops her arm through mine and pulls me further inside what appears to be a formal sitting room that sits just off the foyer.

"I'm not very good at telling that man no," I say loud enough so Gavin can hear, throwing him a playful glare as he steps into the room next to me.

"Where's Deck?" He turns his attention to Kimber.

"Your mom has him fixing a loose cabinet in the kitchen," she says. "I didn't know he was so handy. Man's been holding out on me." She nudges my hip with hers.

"That's because he's smart," Gavin teases, stepping to the side with just enough time to avoid being smacked by Kimber who misses him completely and catches nothing but air.

"You watch yourself, Porter." She wags her finger at him. "Come on. Rosie is dying to meet you." She winks, pulling me through the sitting room and down a short hallway that opens up into a rather large kitchen.

My eyes barely make it past the large island that sits in the center of the room before they land on a petite, auburn-haired lady, her focus firmly on Decklan as he drills a screw into the cabinet hinge.

"There," he says when he's finished, pulling on the door to show her that the issue has been fixed.

"Thank you, my boy." She smiles fondly at Decklan, patting his shoulder. "Don't know what I'd do without you boys." She turns, for the first time seeing that Gavin and I have arrived.

"Speaking of my boys." She smiles

widely at her son, immediately crossing the space toward him.

She has to be a good foot shorter than him and probably half of his weight, but that doesn't stop her from pulling him down to her level as she wraps her arms around his neck and gives him a tight hug.

"So glad you could make it," she says, taking a step back to look at him moments after releasing him from her embrace.

"Mom," he says, turning his eyes toward me which draws her attention in my direction, "I'd like you to meet Harlee."

Her face immediately lights up as she turns toward me, eyes that match Gavin's instantly finding my gaze.

"My dear, you are simply gorgeous," she says moments before pulling me into a hug as well.

I try not to tense at the contact but can't help my natural reaction to do just that. I'm not used to being around such affectionate people. I'm pretty sure I can count the times my mother hugged me on one hand. To have someone offer such affection right out of the gate is a bit overwhelming.

"I'm so glad you could come," she says, releasing me from her embrace before taking both of my hands in hers. "Gavin has told me all about you. He's quite taken with you. Of course, now I can see why." She winks, releasing my hands.

"Ignore her," Gavin interrupts, shaking his head at his mom. "She gets really excited when she gets to meet new people. It's like bringing home a new puppy; she can't help but love all over it."

"Did you just compare me to a dog?" I hit him with a playful glare.

"And she has sass." Rosie pulls my attention back to her. "I think you're gonna fit in here just fine." She winks, turning her attention back to Gavin. "Why don't you and Decklan go set the table? Leave the girls alone for a bit to chit chat," she says, shooing Gavin toward the door.

He throws me an apologetic smile before disappearing into the dining room with Decklan. While normally I would probably be panicking over the prospect of being left alone with his mother, there is something about her that just puts me at ease.

"Is there something I can help with?" I ask, gesturing to the bread and various other ingredients spread out across the counter.

"That would be lovely, dear." She smiles and nods, turning her attention back toward the food. "Kimber, will you cut some cucumber for the salad?" she asks, turning to set two large cucumbers on the island in front of Kimber.

"You got it." Kimber grabs the vegetables

and immediately crosses to the sink to wash them. It's clear that this is not the first time she has helped Rosie in the kitchen.

"Harlee, if you could grab a tomato over there and slice it up for the sandwiches." She points to a row of tomatoes that line the back of the counter. If I had to guess, I would say they were pulled fresh from a garden within the last day or two. I don't how I know that but I can just tell.

"Of course." I cross the space, grabbing the largest of the tomatoes before turning back to Rosie.

"Knives are over there." She nods to the opposite end of the countertop before I can even open my mouth to ask. "And there's an extra cutting board in that cabinet." Again she gestures with her head, dropping two pieces of bread onto the sandwich grill in front of her.

The three of us fall into a steady rhythm, working together in comfortable silence as we prepare lunch. Rosie pauses here and there from what she's doing to ask me a question: what I'm studying in school, where I grew up; the usual basic things. I find it almost unsettling how comfortable she has managed to make me feel in such a short period of time.

It's clear to see I'm not the only one, either. Kimber, who usually is more standoffish than I am, laughs and moves around the kitchen like she's done so a million times before. I have to remind myself that while Kimber had both of her parents growing up; she's never really known what it means to have a *real* mom.

Hell, her mom was a lot worse than mine in some ways. While mine was addicted to pills and absent for most of my childhood, Kimber's spent her early years trying to force her to be someone they wanted as a daughter rather than loving her for the amazing girl she already is. I'm not sure what's worse—having a mom who chooses not to love you for you or having a mom who chooses to love something else more.

Watching the way Kimber interacts with Rosie, it's clear to see that she has come to look at her as more than just Gavin's mom. In a way, the thought makes me jealous. Not that Kimber is a part of Gavin's family now; that makes me extremely happy for her. It's more of what Gavin has—what they all have— that makes me so envious.

I try to picture what Gavin's life must have been like as a child. How it felt having someone like Rosie as a mom and a household full of people who loved him. When I close my eyes I can almost see it; the picture perfect family I used to dream about when I was younger. He had it, all of it. And even though he lost his father a couple of years ago, the amount of love and happiness still evident in this house is overwhelming.

"Harlee." Kimber's voice pulls me from my thoughts, and I look up to see her studying me curiously, a large salad bowl in her hands. "Come on." She gestures to the doorway.

"Oh sorry." I shake my head.

Grabbing the pitcher of iced tea in front of me, I follow her into the dining room that sits just off the kitchen. When we enter the room, Gavin and Decklan are already at the table having a casual conversation with Paxton who must have just arrived. I smile when he nods in my direction, setting the pitcher of tea in the center of the table.

Before I can even turn, I feel Gavin's hand close down around my wrist and tug me sideways. I have no choice but to slide into the chair next to him, hitting him with an annoyed smirk the moment I do.

He raises his eyebrows mischievously, leaning in to rub his nose along my jaw. Paxton groans playfully next to us, turning his attention to Rosie as she enters the room.

"You outdid yourself, Mrs. P." He looks out over the table as Rosie sets a fresh batch of oatmeal cookies in the center of it.

The entire surface is covered with various foods. From grilled turkey club sandwiches and salad to tomato basil soup and croissants, there is a little something to satisfy just about anyone's tastes.

"I know who I'm feeding." She gives Paxton a knowing grin. "I swear you three have been eating me out of house and home for the past fifteen years." She shakes her head, pulling out the chair at the head of the table.

"And yet you keep inviting us back." Decklan laughs, dropping an arm around Kimber's shoulder when she takes a seat next to him.

"What can I say?" Rosie shrugs. "I guess I'm glutton for punishment." She pauses, looking around the table. "Well, what are you all waiting for...? Eat." She gestures to all the food on the table.

Everyone begins helping themselves as conversation flows around the table. Rosie scolds Gavin for missing their monthly spaghetti dinner. Paxton harps on Decklan about when he's going to stop living above the bar and buy a real house, to which Decklan reminds him that he has no room to talk, given that he's living with Gavin.

The bickering and playful banter that floats around me is unlike anything I have ever experienced. I have never met such a different group of people and yet every single one of them fits together to form this beautiful, chaotic mess of a family.

"Everything okay?" Gavin leans in, squeezing my leg gently under the table when he notices I haven't eaten much of my food.

"Yeah." I smile, meeting his incredible blue eyes. "Better than okay." I lay my hand on top of his. "Thank you for bringing me." I keep my voice low as to not pull attention from the other conversations happening around us.

"Thank you for coming." He gives me a half smile that instantly causes my heart to plummet into the bottom of my stomach.

I don't think I will ever get used to how intensely this man affects me.

"Gavin, have you spoken to that sister of yours?" Rosie interrupts the moment, pulling her son's attention to her.

"Which one?" he asks, reaching across the table to retrieve a cookie, taking a large bite the moment it reaches his lips.

"Charlie," she answers like it should be obvious.

"Doesn't she live here?" Gavin asks, taking another bite of his cookie, reminding me more of a young boy than the strong, powerful man I know he is.

"Don't answer my question with another question. You know how much I hate that," she scolds, wagging her finger at him as she reaches for her glass of tea.

"I haven't seen her." He shrugs, finishing off his cookie in one more large bite. "Why do you ask?"

"Well she was out all night with friends

last night but she said she'd be here for lunch. I wasn't sure if maybe you had spoken to her."

The sound of chair legs scraping against the floor pulls my attention to the opposite end of the table just in time to see Paxton stand, grabbing his plate from the table.

"That girl changes her mind on a dime." Gavin shrugs, paying no mind to Paxton as he exits into the kitchen without looking at anyone.

I glance around the table, curious as to how the person who knows him the least seems to be the only one who picks up on the fact that something is off with him. I suspected there was something between Paxton and Charlie the first time I was around them, and seeing his reaction when Rosie said she stayed out all night with friends, only further solidifies that I was right to come to that assumption. Though it would appear that I'm alone in this revelation, considering no one has even reacted to his sudden departure from the table.

"Is she enrolling at the University this spring?" Kimber redirects the conversation slightly.

"She's still undecided." Rosie wipes her mouth on her napkin before dropping it onto the empty plate in front of her. "Honestly, I'm just glad she's home. Having my baby all the way across the country was harder than I thought it would be. Now that all my children are back in the same state, I feel like I can breathe again."

Just like that the conversation shifts in another direction, Rosie turning her attention to Kimber as she asks about how she's enjoying the semester. I swear I have never been around a group of people that can fill the silence with so many different topics in the matter of one meal.

Paxton reappears after a few minutes. He rejoins the table, his expression giving nothing away about where he went or why he left so abruptly. Like he never left at all, he joins in the conversation without skipping a beat.

I don't so much participate as much as I just sit back and listen, watching everyone. I'm still trying to figure out where I fit into this group and if I even belong at all. I jump slightly when my phone springs to life in my back pocket, the sound of high pitch chiming filling the room. I thought I had put it on silent.

"Sorry," I say, scrambling to get it out of my pocket so I can silence it.

I fumble with the button, finally shutting the ringer off. It isn't until then that I even pay attention to the name flashing across the screen.

Bryan.

I immediately flip my gaze to Gavin who is looking directly at me. I suck in a ragged inhale, panic flooding my insides when I realize that not only did he see who was calling my phone, but he also seems to know exactly what that means...

Chapter Eighteen

Gavin

It takes everything I have to get through the remainder of lunch without losing my shit. Why the fuck would that asshat be calling her phone? And why the fuck did she look like she saw a ghost when she realized I had seen it was him calling?

I have trouble focusing on the road as I weave in and out of the late afternoon traffic headed back toward the university. Harlee sits completely silent next to me, staring out the window.

I open my mouth to say something several times on the ten-minute drive back to her dorm, but I want to be able to look at her when she tells me what I know is coming. I'm not a fucking idiot; if Bryan calling didn't give it away, her reaction sure as shit did.

"Gavin, I..." Harlee stumbles out as I pull into the parking lot just a few yards from her dorm building.

"You what?" I ask, shoving the truck into park before killing the engine. "What, Harlee?" I push when she makes no attempt to finish her sentence.

She unlatches her seatbelt and turns toward me, pulling her left leg underneath her on the seat as she does. She holds my gaze for a long moment, clearly not sure where she should start.

"Speak." My annoyance is clear in my voice and I don't miss the way her eyes widen slightly at my dog-like command.

I hate how frustrated I feel. It guts me honestly; to feel the way I feel about her and now to have those feelings obscured by anger. On one hand, I want to pull her into my lap and forget that she lied to me about ending things with Bryan. On the other, I know if I don't hear the truth directly from her, I won't be able to let this go.

"You have to understand, I tried..." she starts, her words falling away when a vicious laugh rips from my chest.

"Let me guess. You tried to break things off with him, but you just couldn't do it." I mimic her demeanor. "Why don't you try a different angle because that sob bullshit might work on *some* men," I say, my referral to Bryan very clear. "But it doesn't fucking fly with me."

"Oh my god, would you stop?" Harlee finally seems to find her voice, her arms crossing in front of her chest as she straightens her posture. "Seriously, you're acting like a fucking child," she snaps, narrowing her eyes at me.

"That's rich." I let out a frustrated sigh, running my hands through my hair.

"Just let me explain," she continues as if I said nothing at all.

"Explain what exactly?" I cock my head to the side to study her. "Explain how you flat out lied to me when I asked you if you had ended things with Bryan?"

"I didn't lie," she insists. "Things are over with Bryan. I just... I just haven't exactly told him that yet."

"You're un-fucking-believable you know that?" I cut in before she can continue.

"I'm trying to make you understand," she tries again.

"Please, by all means, *try* to make me understand." I roll my eyes, already over this entire fucking situation.

"I met Bryan for dinner on Tuesday," she starts, ignoring the look of pure rage that takes over my face. "I only agreed because I wanted to end things face to face," she quickly adds. "But when I got to the restaurant, I just couldn't do it." She hits me with an apologetic look.

"And." I try to keep my emotions in check and keep an open mind. The task is proving much harder than I ever thought possible.

"He had orchestrated this whole special evening to celebrate our two month anniversary. He went through so much trouble to make it happen and was so excited to surprise me that I didn't have the heart to just end it right there on the spot."

"So you just pretended like everything was normal?" I hit her with a look of disbelief. "You had spent the entire weekend in my bed."

"I know. I know. I'm a horrible person." She takes a deep breath, her gaze darting between me and her hands which are knotted tightly in her lap. "It's one thing to break up with someone; it's another to do it when they have clearly gone through so much trouble to show you how important you are to them."

"Did something happen between the two of you?" I brace myself for an answer I'm not sure I want to know.

"We kissed," she admits, her voice barely breaking the surface.

"Are you fucking kidding me?" I roar, the last shred of the hold on my temper tearing away.

Just the thought of that asshole touching her sends an entirely different kind of anger through me. A jealousy I have never experienced before. I don't just hate the way it makes me feel, I loathe it. Every single fucking little part of it.

"It was just a kiss, it meant nothing," she scrambles, clearly caught off guard by my reaction.

"Just a kiss?" I ponder her statement for a long moment, floored by how casual this seems to be to her. "Is this some kind of fucking game to you? See how far you can string us both along and which one is willing to let you do it the longest?"

"Of course not," she gasps.

"Are you sure? Because it sure as hell seems that way to me. Just a kiss... You are a real piece of work you know that?" I shake my head, not sure how to reel my emotions in.

"Me?" Her voice rises in anger. "What about you? You're the one who pursued me, remember? You knew I had a boyfriend. I never tried to hide that from you. What the hell gives you the right to treat me like some unfaithful whore? *You* are not the one I've been cheating on, Bryan is. Me kissing him was not a betrayal to you. Me being with you was the betrayal to him. So stop acting like I've committed some unforgivable act that you just can't get past. You asked for this," she screams, pointing her finger in my face. "You forced me to love you when all I wanted was to forget you ever existed."

I open my mouth but then close it again, the reality of her words hitting me like a thousand pound brick. It settles on my chest and makes it feel damn near impossible to suck in a full breath.

"You're angry with me, but really it should be me angry with you," she continues, a welling tear finally finding its way from the corner of her eye. It rolls down her cheek slowly, leaving a wet trail down her perfect skin.

It takes everything in me not to pull her into my arms and comfort her, but I know nothing will get resolved that way.

"Do you have any idea the position you've put me in?" She swipes at a second tear. "I was finally happy and then you had to push your way back into my life and fuck everything up." Her voice breaks in the middle.

"I didn't realize I was such an imposition on your perfect little fucking life," I bite, the overwhelming rush I felt moments earlier fizzing away in an instant.

"That's not what I meant." She

immediately backpedals.

"I know what you meant, Harlee; you've been more than fucking clear," I bite.

"Don't do that." She reaches for my hand, her tears falling harder when I rip it out of her grasp. "Don't you dare pull away from me, Gavin Porter. You're not imposing on my life. You *are* my life. I just need you to understand this isn't so black and white. I had a life before you, a boyfriend, and he deserves the best I can do by him given what I've done. I refuse to cause him any unnecessary pain. I won't. I'm sorry if you can't understand that."

"Oh, I understand it just fine. The problem is that you seem to care more about hurting him than hurting me."

"I haven't done anything to you." She tries to control the tremble in her voice.

"You're fucking blind if you believe that's true. You've been stringing me along the exact same way you have Bryan. You're not willing to let either of us go, and I'm not a man who can share."

"I'm not stringing you along, Gavin. I chose you. I choose you. I know what I want." She wipes at another tear that falls down her cheek.

"Then prove it," I challenge. "Call Bryan, right now. Tell him exactly what's been going on between us and end this once and for all."

"You can't be serious." She shakes her

head.

"Oh, I'm very serious."

"That would devastate him," she objects.

"And?" I question. "He deserves the truth, Harlee."

"I understand that, but there is a right way to do this," she insists.

"And what exactly is the right way, Harlee?" I bite. "To tell him you just need some time apart. That it's not him, it's you. What bullshit excuse are you planning to feed the poor bastard?"

"Whatever one hurts him the least."

"Not an option." I shake my head slowly back and forth. "He deserves the truth, Harlee. And I deserve someone who is willing to do whatever it takes to be with me."

"I am willing to do whatever it takes to be with you. I put myself in this mess to begin with because of you. Now you act like I somehow made you false promises and misled you. You blew me off after we slept together the first time. You dropped me so quick I didn't even have time to wash your smell off my skin before you were moving on to the next girl in line. You can't blame me for not wanting to end things with Bryan when you suddenly reappeared in my life."

"Do you even hear yourself? You're openly admitting that you cheated on Bryan and yet still kept him around in case I flaked.

What does that say about you, Harlee?"

"You think I don't know what kind of person this makes me? You think I don't feel guilty every second of every day? I do. I hate the person that looks back at me in the mirror. But you can't fault me for not wanting to lose Bryan over someone like you."

"Someone like me?" I question, letting it hang between us for several long seconds.

"Don't act like you have no idea what I'm talking about. I've seen the way you are with women. I'm not stupid. I knew what kind of man you were from the very first night I saw you. I had a good thing with Bryan; a stable thing. I was determined not to let you derail that. But then you'd smile at me or kiss me and my entire fucking mind would turn to mush. I didn't want to want you, Gavin. I didn't want to love you. I wanted to hate you because hating you is so much fucking easier. You did this. You put all three of us in this situation. So don't sit here and lecture me about the kind of person I am. You pursued another man's girlfriend, and you did so without any remorse."

"Because I go for what I fucking want, and I don't let anything or *anyone* stand in my way."

"That's an easy mentality to adopt when you're not the one who has to break someone else's heart," she snaps, clearly growing more frustrated.

"I get the hesitation in the beginning, I do. I understand why you tried to resist me. Hell, I even understand why you chose not to end things with Bryan right away. But it has been weeks now, Harlee. Have I not proven to you that I'm in this and this is what I want?" I gesture between the two of us.

"It's not that simple. What you're asking me to do isn't fair. I can't just call him and drop this on him. Why hurt him unnecessarily? You win. You've got me. Now let me do this in a way that I can still live with myself afterward."

"You mean let you sit on it for who knows how much longer before you fill the poor bastard's mind with lies and false hope. He deserves to know the truth, Harlee. He deserves to know what's going on. Otherwise, he'll never let you go. He will pine after you and hold out hope that you will change your mind and come back to him."

"No, he won't." I'm not sure if she's trying to convince me or herself.

"I've met the guy, Harlee. I've seen how he looks at you. You go to him with some bullshit about things just not working, and he'll never settle. You go to him and tell him the truth..."

"He'll never want to see me again." She finishes my sentence. "And that's exactly what you want. You want me to unnecessarily cause him pain so you don't have to worry about him being a factor anymore."

"Of course, I don't want to fucking deal with him still pining after you. I want him as far away from both of us as possible. But you misunderstand my request as selfish; it's not. You call Bryan and tell him the truth because that's what decent human beings do."

"So now I'm not a decent person because I don't want to hurt someone?" She's looking at me like I have five heads.

"Call him." I ignore her question.

"And if I don't?"

"Then we're done," I say, matter of fact.

"You can't be serious." I see the panic and realization flood her face in unison.

"I'm very serious. I need to know that you're with me one hundred percent."

"I am. I am with you a hundred percent. Please, just don't make me do it this way." Tears flood her cheeks and she reaches for me again.

"You say you've made your choice, then prove it," I say, reaching around her to pull her cell phone out of her back pocket. "Show me it's me." I flip her hand upward and set the device in her palm.

She stares at it for several long moments before her tear-filled gaze meets mine.

"I can't." Her words are barely a whisper

and yet echo over and over again like she's screaming at the top of her lungs.

"You mean you won't." I keep my voice even despite that fact that I feel like I could punch a fucking hole straight through one of the truck windows at this current moment.

"If you could just give me more..."

"You can have all the fucking time you want," I interrupt her. "I'm done," I say, turning forward as I reach for the ignition, firing the truck to life.

"What are you saying?"

"I'm saying get the fuck out of my truck, Harlee." I keep my eyes focused forward as I try to hold my shit together.

"Gavin. Don't do this," she pleads, her hand settling down on top of my forearm.

I shake off her touch and finally meet her gaze.

"I said, get the fuck out of my truck," I repeat, accentuating each word. "Now." My voice booms through the truck causing Harlee to jump slightly.

I grip the steering wheel tighter and focus my eyes back through the windshield.

"For what it's worth," she says weakly, shoving open the passenger door. "I love you."

I ignore both the sting and elation that crashes over me at her words. I can feel my emotions slip behind the black wall, numbness taking the place of where my love and anger reside.

"You have a funny way of showing people that you love them," I grind out.

I hear her trying to muffle a sob as she slams the door shut and takes off toward her dorm. I watch as she crosses the courtyard before finally disappearing inside the large brick building.

I know I'm an asshole. I know I have no right to demand such things of her. I know I don't deserve her love. I know a lot, but it doesn't change one fucking thing. She's proven to me she's incapable of handling this on her own which means only one thing. I'm either going to have to force her into a situation she can't back out of, or I'm simply going to have to let her go.

Either way, I will most likely end up losing her in the end...

Chapter Nineteen

<u>Gavin</u>

"You know, she's just as miserable as you are." Kimber slides into the stool next to me.

"I don't know what the fuck you're talking about." I keep my gaze focused on the flat screen television mounted on the wall behind the bar, taking another long drink of my beer.

"Are you sure you and Decklan aren't *real* brothers?" She nudges my shoulder with hers. "You sure as hell act the same."

"He just likes to be like me." I turn my face, finally meeting her gaze.

"There he is." She smiles, causing my

own lips to twitch upward in the closest thing to a smile I have formed in the last forty-eight hours.

"Where is Decklan anyway?" I look around the bar, realizing he must not have come down with her.

"He's sleeping." Her statement causes me to glance at the clock.

"At ten thirty?" I gape at her.

"I know, right," she laughs. "For the longest time, I couldn't get him to sleep at all. Now I feel like it's a struggle to keep him awake some nights."

"He's an old man now." I laugh before falling serious. "I don't think I've ever thanked you," I say, not missing the confusion that immediately floods her face.

"Thanked me?" she questions.

"For what you've done for Deck. You pulled him out of a hole I was convinced he would eventually die in. You've given him life. I don't think I've ever seen him so happy. I know things were rocky there for a while. I'm glad you stuck it out."

"Please. That man is stuck with me whether he wants to be or not." She smiles, the action lighting up her entire face. "You don't have to thank me, though. I love him."

"I know I don't have to thank you, but I'm doing so anyway. He's my family and now so are you." I nudge her shoulder the same way she did mine just moments ago.

"I take it you've spoken to her?" I pull the conversation back to Harlee without skipping a beat.

I can try to play it off like I don't care all I want. It still doesn't change the fact that it's fucking killing me to try to focus on anything other than the beautiful girl that has completely consumed every fucking inch of me.

"I have," she confirms, nodding to Val when she slides a glass of water in front of her.

All I can see is Harlee's face, the events of two nights ago replaying in my head like a bad movie I just can't seem to force myself to shut off. I thought I was doing the right thing. I thought forcing her hand would somehow prove that I had won, that I was who she wanted. Unfortunately, it would seem my actions have had the opposite effect.

She's made no attempt to contact me, and I'm too fucking proud to make the first move. I'm not exactly sure where that leaves us.

"How is she?" I ask when she makes no attempt to elaborate on her statement.

"How do you think she is?" She narrows her gaze on me.

"I guess it's safe to say I've made a real mess of things." I shake my head, turning my focus forward.

"So it would seem," she agrees, falling silent for a long moment. "What did you hope to prove anyway?"

"I don't know." I shrug, taking another long drink of beer. "I guess I just hoped she'd stop finding excuses not to commit to me."

"Do you blame her?" Her question pulls my gaze back to her face. I expect to see a look of judgment or at the very least one of distaste; what I see instead is understanding.

"I get it, Gavin," she continues. "You love her. You're ready for more. But you have to understand that for a girl like Harlee, *more* can be a very scary thing. Especially when it's with someone like you." She laughs when I arch my eyebrows. "Relax, I don't mean that in a bad way. You know I love you."

"Why do I get the feeling a *but* is about to come out of your mouth."

"But." She laughs before continuing. "You aren't the most open person in the world, and you do have a bit of a reputation as a player." She seems almost apologetic by her statement. "Did you ever consider that this was never about Bryan? That Bryan was just Harlee's way of buying herself more time where you're concerned?"

"Is that what she told you?" I question.

"She hasn't told me anything. Not really." She shrugs. "I don't even know if she's figured this out for herself yet. But I know her well enough to know when she's stalling." She pauses, clearly choosing her next words wisely. "Has she ever told you about her parents? About her childhood?"

"Bits and pieces. I know her mom passed. I know her dad lives close by. I know she doesn't have any siblings. Is there something else?" I ask, seeing the look of realization as it crosses her face.

"Gavin, Harlee's mom didn't just die, she overdosed. She was a drug addict. And what's worse, Harlee is the one who found her. Can you imagine being ten-years-old and walking in to find your mother sprawled out on the floor no longer breathing?"

"I had no idea," I admit, trying to calm the sudden rush of sadness I feel at the thought.

"And her dad does live close by, as in Oregon State Penitentiary close." She ignores my clear surprise and continues. "When Harlee was fifteen, he was arrested for armed robbery and sentenced to ten years."

"Why wouldn't she tell me this?" I question, confused and honestly a little hurt that I have to hear this from Kimber instead of Harlee herself.

"Is that something you would walk around announcing, especially to someone you're falling in love with? She's embarrassed, Gavin. Her aunt Joy took her in afterward.

Her father's much younger sister," she clarifies. "Joy has been more of a mom to Harlee in the last four years than her real mom ever was. But this isn't a sad story, Gavin. I'm not trying to spin you some tail about how horrible her childhood was. I'm just trying to give you a better understanding of where she comes from. She has a harder time trusting than most, and I've found that she tends to make excuses when it comes to committing herself to anything. I think at the end of the day, she's just afraid to open herself up to the unpredictability of a real relationship."

"Yet she's with Bryan?" I interject.

"And look at that relationship." She rolls her eyes. "If she felt even half for Bryan what she feels for you, she never would have even looked at another man, let alone be sleeping with one on the side. Bryan is safe for her. He's kind and sweet and doesn't ask too much of her. Deep down she knows he can't hurt her because she doesn't love him. Instead, he's her armor. She's hiding behind him."

"So when I asked her to shed her armor..." I start.

"She panicked." Kimber finishes my sentence. "I don't doubt that she likes Bryan, but I knew almost immediately that their relationship stemmed from her feelings for you. I knew it when she suddenly went from obsessing over you to dating him out of the blue. Harlee hasn't ever really had a steady relationship, at least not from what she's told me. And then all of a sudden she's dating some guy, whose direction she wouldn't even look in a few weeks ago. And it all lines up with when you came into her life. I refuse to believe that's just coincidence. Bryan is more her shield than her actual boyfriend."

"I don't get it, though. Why shield herself from me, if that's what she's actually doing? I've been nothing but upfront with her. She knows what I want." I finish off my beer before sliding the glass to the edge of the bar. "I'm not playing her. I'm not playing games. I fucking love the girl."

"I know you do." She reaches out, patting my forearm with her hand. "But take it from someone who's been there, loving a man is hard enough; loving someone you're convinced will eventually break your heart is something else entirely. It's hard to really put yourself out there when you're certain you already know the outcome."

"Then why choose to love that person at all?" I ask, nodding when Val slides a fresh beer across the bar to me.

"Because it's not a choice. Did you choose to love Harlee?"

"No," I answer truthfully.

"Exactly. It just happens. Harlee loves

you, Gavin. I know you know that. You are who she wants. I know you know that, too. But you can't force her into something she's not ready for. All you can do is show her that she's worth waiting for."

"Like you did with Decklan," I state, knowing first-hand how determined this girl was when it came to holding on to Deck no matter how hard he tried to push her away.

"In a way, yes. I knew he loved me. I also knew he was going through something I didn't fully understand. Don't get me wrong, there were times that I wanted to walk away. Times when I convinced myself that life without him would simply be easier. But at the end of the day, easy was never what I wanted. I wanted him. No matter how many ups and downs we had, no matter how many secrets he kept or how often I wanted to force them out of him. Not one of those things made me love him any less. In fact, they made me love him more. That's how I knew it was real. There was nothing I wasn't willing to sacrifice for his happiness, and there still isn't. That's what love is really all about. Wanting what's best for the other person even if it directly conflicts with your own happiness."

"But what happens when the person's happiness you value above your own is being restricted by themselves? What if they are standing in the way of their own happiness and are just too blind to realize it? What then?" I spin my stool slightly so that I can face Kimber straight on.

"Then I guess it's your job to make them see it." Her response is instant. "But just make sure that you're doing it for her and not for yourself."

"What if I'm doing it for both?"

"Why do I get the feeling you're planning something?" she questions, her pretty face turning suddenly accusatory.

"Because I am."

"I say this because I love both of you. Be careful. Even when you set out to do things for the right reason, it can still blow up in your face. You have to make sure you can live with either outcome."

"I won't live without her. Honestly, I don't fucking know if I can."

"Then you better make damn sure you know what you're doing," she warns.

"Fuck. I don't know anything when it comes to that girl," I admit.

"Funny, she said the same thing about you."

"I thought when I demanded that she call Bryan with me sitting next to her that she would. I thought for sure when she refused that she'd eventually agree. I thought when I pushed her away it would make her see just how serious I am about this, and she would realize I was right. You see how well that's worked out." I sigh, drinking half of my beer in one large gulp before setting the glass back onto the bar.

"Hell, now she probably wants nothing to fucking do with me," I tack on.

"That couldn't be further from the truth."

"Why do you say that?" I ask when she makes no attempt to explain.

"Harlee hasn't called you, but that's not because she hasn't wanted to. She truly believes she's pushed you too far and you're done with her. She spent so much time convincing herself that eventually you would walk away; once you did, I think she just accepted that there wasn't anything she could do to change it."

"Fuck. I really fucked this one up, didn't I?" I rest my elbows against the bar, dropping my head into my hands.

"I actually see where you were coming from. It can't be easy loving someone you feel like you have to share with someone else. I'm surprised you've let it go on as long as you have."

"I was trying to win her heart before I forced her hand."

"Well, you've definitely won her heart. Question is, what are you going to do now?"

"Force her hand." I let out a small laugh

when Kimber cocks a brow.

"Didn't you try that already?" She shakes her head at me. "How's that working out for you again?"

"This time, it won't be me demanding the answers." I sit back, turning my head toward Kimber.

"I don't think I want to know," she says, shaking her head.

"Good, because I have no intention of telling you." My words cause her eyes to go wide just moments before we both start laughing.

"My god, I don't know how Harlee deals with you." She laughs out, turning her attention to the door just to the right of the bar when it swings open and Decklan steps out.

He yawns and runs a hand through his messy hair, smiling when he catches sight of me and Kimber sitting at the bar.

"There you are," he says the moment he reaches us, dropping a kiss on the top of Kimber's head before throwing me a nod.

"What are you doing up?" Kimber asks, swiveling her stool so that she is facing him.

"I woke up and you weren't there. I couldn't seem to go back to sleep after that." He shrugs, not even trying to hide the fact that this girl completely fucking owns him.

I know the feeling.

"Sorry, I wasn't tired. Found this sorry sap drinking away his sorrows, so I thought I'd keep him company." She throws a playful wink in my direction.

"Is that so?" Decklan turns his attention toward me. "Anything I can do?" he asks, already knowing in full detail the events that took place after I left my mom's with Harlee the day before yesterday.

"Probably best to leave this to the professionals," Kimber chimes in jokingly, sliding out of her stool to stand next to Decklan. "Come on, let's get you back to bed." She links her arm through his.

"I'm not really tired anymore." He smiles down at her.

"Who said anything about sleeping." She laughs when the realization of what she's saying finally seems to sink in.

"Night, dude." Deck briefly lays a hand on my shoulder before throwing his arm around Kimber.

"Good luck," Kimber speaks over her shoulder as Decklan leads her away. "And don't make things worse." She raises her voice as she gets further away.

"I'll do my best," I holler back, laughing as her and Decklan disappear upstairs.

Chapter Twenty

<u>Harlee</u>

I have no idea why the hell I'm doing this. I should have just ignored Kimber's phone call, and continued to pretend like my life isn't falling apart around me. But something made me answer it. Now here I am, driving two hours to Portland despite how late in the evening it is.

I just couldn't stop myself after hearing what Kimber had to say. I have to see him, now. I have to explain to him why I couldn't do what he asked of me. I know it isn't unreasonable. I should break things off with Bryan. It's what's best for everyone involved. But I just couldn't do it. Not like that. Not with him breathing down my neck and listening to every word.

He was so angry with me. I don't think I've ever had a man look at me the way Gavin looked at me that night. It was like part of him wanted to strip me bare and the other wanted to punch me in the face. The contradicting emotions made things more than a little difficult to read.

I've spent two days trying to convince myself that getting out of that truck and letting him drive away was the right move even though it's the last thing I wanted.

I'm done now. Being without him these past couple of days, not hearing his voice or his laugh, not feeling the warmth of him pressed up against me, has been enough to make me realize that some things are just worth sacrificing everything for.

He is worth everything and then some. I think it's about time I tell him this.

I call Bryan four times on my way to *Deviants*, but still haven't reached him by the time I pull into the parking lot behind the bar just after one in the morning. I guess I shouldn't be surprised. I have been completely avoiding him since we went to dinner last week. As far as I know he's probably planning on ending things with me and all of this back and forth trying to save his feelings will have been for not.

I decide to try and call one more time before going inside to see Gavin. But like the other four times I've called, the phone goes straight to voicemail. This time, I decide to leave a message.

"Hey Bryan, it's me. Listen, we need to talk. Can you call me back when you get this?" I disconnect the call, killing the engine to Joy's Mercedes as soon as I pull into a spot at the back of the lot.

I tried returning the car to her last week only to find out she took an impromptu trip to the Florida Keys for a week and won't be home until the day after tomorrow. Now I'm glad I decided to keep it until she gets back, otherwise this trip wouldn't have really been an option. I'm not like Kimber. I can't endure a two-hour cab ride to Portland.

Taking a deep breath, I exit the car, tightening my coat around my shoulders as I make the cold walk around the building to the front entrance of the bar. I wish I had taken more time to get ready but this truly was a spur of the moment, now or never kind of thing, so Gavin's just going to have to deal with my leggings and oversized tunic. I'm sure I look every bit a hot mess, and I'm also sure that I really don't give a shit right now.

Given that it's one of their slower nights, there is no bouncer manning the front door, and I'm able to walk directly inside without drawing any attention to my arrival. It's no secret that Gavin and I have been hanging out and everyone that works here knows exactly who I am.

I slide my coat off and drape it over my arm the moment I step inside, the warmth of the bar a complete contrast to the bitter night air outside. I look around the room, scanning the faces of only a handful of customers before finally turning my attention to the female bartender who seems to notice my arrival instantly.

"Hey Val," I say the moment I reach the bar. She barely looks up from where she's washing glasses to give me a brief nod. "Is Gavin still here or has he already left for the night?"

"Um..." She gives me a puzzled look and then gestures to her left drawing my attention to two people at the end of the bar.

It takes me a moment to recognize Gavin, not because he looks any different but because his face is almost completely hidden behind a big breasted, slender brunette that is practically sitting in his lap.

I ignore the sting of jealousy that floods through me as I set off in their direction, not really sure what's going on until I get close enough to hear them.

"Oh come on, Gav. You used to be so much fun." The woman whines, grinding against his leg.

"And he used to not have a girlfriend." I step up next to them, my eyes locking immediately with Gavin's, which go wide the moment he registers my face.

"Girlfriend?" The brunette pulls my attention to her as she steps up in front of me. "You? Please." She throws her head back and laughs, the sound slurred through her clear intoxication.

"As opposed to a catch like you," I bite sarcastically, my nostrils flaring slightly.

I've never been in a real fight in my entire life, but given the amount of adrenaline pumping through me at the current moment, I have no doubt I could knock this bitch on her ass and not even break a sweat.

"Now, ladies," Gavin chimes in, pulling both of our gazes to him as he stands, stepping between us. "It was good seeing you again, Abbey," he says to the brunette. "Val will get you a cab when you're ready to leave." He turns, ignoring her clear disappointment as his attention comes to me.

"As for you, come with me." His tone is harsh and clipped as his hand closes around mine. In one quick tug, he's pulling me behind him, away from the bar and down the hallway that houses the bathrooms.

At first, I think he's leading me toward the back entrance but then he veers left, pushing his way through the door that leads into a small storage closet where they keep cleaning supplies and other various things stocked.

The room goes pitch black when he slams the door shut just moments after pulling me inside but then the light flickers on, basking us in a dim yellow glow.

"What the fuck are you doing here?" He takes a commanding step toward me causing me to step back.

"I needed to see you," I stutter out, taking another step backward until my back hits the cold steel of the door.

"I thought I was pretty clear the last time we spoke." He steps directly into me, his chest pressing into mine as his face hovers just inches away.

It isn't until now that I notice the alcohol on his breath or the bright red streaks that line his eyes.

"I'm sorry, did I ruin your fun?" I spit, anger creeping through my spine at the thought of what may have happened between him and that woman had I not shown up.

"Maybe you did." His mouth curves into a wicked smile, taunting me.

What happened to the man that Kimber said just two hours ago was beating himself up over the way he treated me? *"He's so in love with you."* She had said. *"You guys really need to work this out.*" She had said.

Well, fuck that.

I have no interest in working anything out with a man who thinks it's okay to dangle other women in front of my face. I should never have come here.

"You're an asshole." I try to push against his body when he presses into me harder, but it's like pushing against a brick wall, and he doesn't move an inch.

"Get off me, Gavin," I warn.

"Or what?" He leans down, his lips so close to mine I can practically taste them. "What are you going to do, Harlee?" He grinds against me, making the presence of his hardening erection known.

I wish my stomach didn't clench tightly at this knowledge. I wish it didn't cause my skin to prickle or little beads of sweat to form at my hairline, but it does. My entire body comes to life in that one action.

Traitor.

"Why are you here?" he growls close to my lips, his hard gaze remaining firmly on me.

"I....I." I can't get the words out. My mind can't form a coherent thought with him so close to me, his smell invading all my senses.

He studies my reaction for a fraction of a second before another wicked smile lights up his face. There is no time for me to react, no time for me to speak. His lips crash down onto mine so suddenly that for a good five seconds I stand completely motionless, my brain unable to process the sudden change in events.

His hands trail down my sides before I feel the material of my shirt being lifted. He breaks away from my mouth just long enough to pull the tunic over my head and toss it somewhere behind him.

My hands go into his hair as his head dips, his lips trailing down my neck, across my chest. Pulling the material of my bra aside, he sucks a nipple into his mouth on one long pull, the sensation causing me to cry out.

I can feel his smile against my damp flesh as he moves to the other nipple, repeating the process. By the time his mouth finds mine again, I am desperate and greedy. I grip the back of his head and kiss him so deeply, I swear there's not an inch of him I can't taste.

"Fuck, I've missed you," he growls against my mouth, his thumbs hitching inside the band of my pants before pulling them and my panties down in one quick tug.

I hear the zipper of his jeans next, followed by the rustle of fabric just before I feel his hard length bare against my stomach. He slides off his shirt before grabbing me at the back of my thighs, lifting me into the air, pinning my back against the door behind me.

"I want to feel you," he groans, sliding his erection between my wet folds.

"Then do it," I speak against his mouth, grinding myself downward.

"Fuck." He slides deep inside of me without another moment of hesitation.

Dropping his face into the crook of my neck, he stills, savoring the feeling of me bare around him.

I run my fingers through the back of his hair, overtaken by this moment of intimacy.

"Look at me." I pull Gavin's face up to meet mine. "I love you," I say, pressing my lips to his.

I don't know why I felt the need to say it. Things are so up in the air with us right now but honestly, that doesn't make my statement any less true. I need him to know that I'm his, that I will always be his.

My statement seems to be his undoing as he deepens the kiss and starts to move beneath me. It's slow at first. He pulls in and out at a snail's pace, making sure I feel every single inch of him. But as the pleasure mounts so does his movements.

Within minutes we are tearing at each other's skin: biting, sucking, licking as he forcefully pounds into me. My body collides with the steel door behind me over and over but I continue to beg him for more; harder, faster, deeper. I want to feel him, all of him.

I'm the first to explode, my orgasm hitting me so suddenly and intensely that I can't control the sound of pleasure that rips from my mouth. It hits me in waves, pulling me under with each one before I'm able to resurface for air.

I can tell by the way Gavin tightens his grip on me that he's there, too. He thrusts inside of me so hard all I can hear is our two bodies slapping together and little spurts of air as we both struggle for breath.

On one deep growl, he spills his release inside of me. The feeling so intense, I feel like my body might come apart again at any second. His movements slow until finally he stops completely, his head dropping to my shoulder as he tries to even his breathing.

We remain like that for several long seconds before he finally pulls out of me and sets me on my feet. My legs wobble slightly under my weight as I work to reassemble my clothing. After locating my shirt thrown across a stack of paper towels, I slide it on and then turn back to face Gavin.

He's fully dressed again, his black shirt clinging to his muscular torso with his faded jeans hanging loosely on his hips. His hair is sticking out in different directions, my fingers running through it over and over again giving it a messy, just woke up kind of look. My god, this man looks like he just stepped out of a modeling magazine. Every single bit of him is pure and complete perfection.

He stalks toward me, each step so slow I wonder if he will ever close the short distance between us. Stopping directly in front of me, he grabs my chin and tilts my face upward, leaning down to hover just inches from my face.

"I love you, too." His whispered words are a complete contrast to the intensity in his eyes, and I all but melt right here on the spot.

Chapter Twenty-one

Harlee

It's still dark when I leave Gavin's condo the next morning. It took everything I had to climb out of his bed and leave him there sleeping but there's no way I could miss class this morning. I've already fallen behind because I've been so distracted. Missing my exam today would only make my situation that much worse.

The traffic is light as I make the two-hour drive back to Eugene. My mind wanders as I watch headlights filter through the darkness. So much has changed over the course of a few short weeks. So many things are different, me being the most prominent difference of all.

Gavin has altered me in a way I never thought possible. I didn't know one person could affect your life on such an epic scale. I thought I knew what I was getting with him. I thought I had him all figured out, but he has turned out to be something I never expected.

I can still hear his voice as he whispered how much he loved me into the early hours of the morning. I can still see his eyes, the way they looked at me like I was the most precious thing in the world. I can still feel his hands, the way they brushed against my skin so gently and yet with so much power.

I am completely and utterly lost to this man.

Now there's only one thing left to do.

Gavin didn't mention Bryan through the course of the night, not even once. While the last thing I wanted was to dredge it up, a part of me still feels in limbo because nothing has really been settled. I felt even worse when I woke up this morning to three missed calls from Bryan, having turned my phone on vibrate before entering the bar last night.

Regardless, I know what I have to do and I have every intention of going back to Portland tonight, this time to tell Gavin I have finally ended it. Because that is exactly what I plan to do today. I know it won't be easy and I know Bryan will be upset, but at the end of the day, I know that dragging this out is only going to make matters worse for everyone involved.

I'm not going to tell him about Gavin. Maybe that makes me an even more despicable human being, but I just don't see why I need to add insult to injury. Is it not bad enough to be broken up with? To add being cheated on to the mix just seems like a blow I don't need to land. It doesn't change anything.

Bryan is an amazing guy and someone I do honestly care about. I want to make this as painless as possible for him. I honestly don't know why I've waited so long. I think in a way hanging on to Bryan gave me an excuse not to commit to Gavin. Because being with Gavin isn't just amazing and wonderful, it's also scary as hell.

My phone buzzes to life on my passenger seat just as I pull into my dorm room parking lot. It's just after seven in the morning so I'm more than a little surprised when I see Angel's name flash across the screen.

"You're up early," I say, holding the device to my ear.

"Ugh. Don't remind me," she groans.

"Wow, don't you sound chipper," I joke. "Long night?"

"You have no idea. Trenton took me to a party at his friend's house last night."

"Oh yeah. How'd that go?" I ask, killing

the engine of the car before leaning back against the seat.

"I haven't been to bed yet. I just got home," she replies on a ridiculous giggle.

"Oh my god, are you still drunk?" I laugh, shaking my head even though she can't see me.

"Maybe a little," she admits. "So there's no way I'm gonna make it to classes. I was wondering if you could send me your notes from Ethics class today," she says, referring to the one and only class we have together this semester.

It's my second class of the morning and starts at eleven.

"Yeah, I can do that," I agree. "Now get some sleep. I'll call you later."

"You're the best." She yawns into the phone. "Love you. Love you."

"Love you, too," I say, ending the call.

****

The morning drags on so slowly that by the time the afternoon rolls around it feels like it should be evening. I think part of it has to do with the dread I feel over talking to Bryan. The other is my excitement to see Gavin after it's all said and done.

Needless to say, the last thing I expect to see when I finally exit my last class of the day just after three o'clock is Gavin. At first, I think I'm imagining things when I see him stand from a bench just outside the building. But then when he walks toward me and flashes me that incredible smile, I know he must be real.

"What are you doing here?" I ask the moment we reach each other.

"You left me this morning." He snags my book bag off my arm and throws it on his shoulder.

The action makes me feel like I'm in high school again and my hot popular boyfriend is carrying my books through the hall. Not that anything like that ever happened to me, but I've seen it in movies a hundred times.

"Sorry. I've missed so much class here recently, and I had a pretty big test this morning." I smile, walking with him when he takes off in the direction of the dorms.

My building is less than a ten-minute walk from this current location and clearly, Gavin knows the way. Having grown up not far from here, I'd say he's been here more than a couple times.

"Did you sleep at all?" He keeps the conversation casual as we stroll across the grounds.

"I got a couple of hours." I shrug. "So you drove all this way because you woke up and I was gone?" I question, finding that reason hard to believe.

"Pretty much." His mouth pulls up into a one-sided grin.

He flashes his eyes down to my face for a brief moment before turning his attention forward again. "I didn't have any plans for the day," he adds.

After a couple minutes of casual back and forth chit chat, I finally decide that I might as well get the hard part over with. Him showing up kinda throws a wrench in my plans to talk to Bryan, but I'm still determined to take care of this today and I want him to know this information.

"Listen, we should probably talk about Bryan." I let out a slow exhale and keep my eyes facing ahead of me.

"O-k-a-y," he drags out, waiting for me to continue.

"I owe you an apology." I stop next to a large tree that sits in the open green space in front of my dorm building, finally meeting his gaze.

"What for?" he asks when I take a long pause.

"I never should have entered into anything with you while I had a boyfriend. It wasn't fair to Bryan and it certainly wasn't fair to you. I just want you to know that I plan to speak with him today."

"I'm sorry ,too." His statement surprises me. "I'm sorry for the way I spoke to you. It wasn't right. I've just never been in a situation like this before. I've never cared enough about a girl to care who or what she's doing when she's not with me. All I knew is I wanted you, I didn't care who I hurt along the way, including you. I don't know the rules here."

"Me either," I answer truthfully.

"All I know is the thought of someone else touching you makes me raving fucking mad." He lets out a gruff laugh. "I can't take it. I can't deal with the way that makes me feel. I won't share you, now or ever."

"And you won't have to," I reassure him, reaching up to cup his face. "I love you, Gavin Porter. So much," I say, pulling his face down toward me.

His lips brush against mine for only a fraction of a second before I hear a throat clear behind me. My entire body freezes and my stomach clenches tightly with dread. I know it's Bryan before I even turn around and look at him.

"So now I know why you've been so distant here recently." His voice is laced with anger. His normal laid back demeanor is nowhere in sight.

I've never seen angry Bryan. I didn't know he was capable of looking at me the way he's looking at me right now.

"Bryan, I can explain," I start, taking a step toward him.

"Explain what, Harlee? How you've been fucking him behind my back?" He bites, gesturing to Gavin who is standing completely still behind me.

"How long?" he continues, his nostrils flaring as he stares daggers at me. "How long have you been fucking him, Harlee?"

"Bryan... I," I start, but he doesn't let me get anything out.

"Don't fucking say it. I can't believe a word that comes out of your mouth. You know I thought I was the luckiest fucking guy in the world when we started dating. I even told my parents how I thought I had finally found the one. What a fucking joke." He lets out a high-pitched laugh that sounds almost devilish.

"And you know the real kicker?" he spits. "Who knows how much longer you would have strung me along; you clearly had no intention of telling me the truth. How long ago was it that we went to dinner? That I told you I loved you? That you let me sit in that restaurant and pour my heart out to you, all the while you were fucking him on the side? Fuck, that was just days ago! Who the fuck does that to another person?"

"I'm so sorry." I try to apologize, fighting back the tears that are welling in my eyes.

I'm sad that I hurt Bryan. I'm upset

about the things he's saying, no matter how true they are. But most of all I'm embarrassed that Gavin is here to witness every last second of it.

"Don't. Don't you dare fucking apologize to me. I won't let you rid yourself of this guilt. I want it to fester. I want you to have face who you are and what you're capable of doing to someone who loved you. I can only imagine what you're in for." He says this last part to Gavin. "Good luck with that." He nods at him and then spins on his heel, disappearing almost as quickly as he had appeared.

My mind swirls as I stare across the grounds, watching him grow further and further away until I can no longer see him at all. His words play over and over in my head, the way he looked at Gavin in almost appreciation making me feel sick to my stomach. It's like he already knew about Gavin well before he saw us kissing just moments ago. Something about what he said just doesn't add up.

Turning to face Gavin, I wipe at the tears flowing down my face.

"You?" I force out in disbelief. "You told him?"

His expression remains completely unreadable. He doesn't deny or admit my accusation, he just simply stands there staring at me.

"Say something," I scream, my voice carrying across the open space, drawing the attention of a couple students exiting the dorm building.

I ignore their curious stares, my eyes locked firmly on Gavin.

"I did what I thought needed to be done at the time." His voice is flat when he finally speaks, but there is regret in his eyes.

"You did what needed to be done?" I question in disbelief. "Did you see him? Did you see what you did to him?" I gesture back to where Bryan was just standing.

"I didn't do that to him. You did." Again his tone is flat, his expression completely hard. "You had a choice that you chose not to make weeks ago."

"You had no right," I start, my tears now turning from guilt to anger.

"I had every right," he snaps, for the first time showing any real emotion at all. "You think he's the only one you've been stringing along? You think he's the only one in this situation that's hurt? After last night, I couldn't do it. I couldn't fucking let this shit go on for even one more day. I got his number from your phone while you were sleeping and I texted him this morning. I didn't tell him any details, only that if he wanted to see for himself where to be and when."

"So you coming here... You orchestrated

this entire fucking thing?" I can't believe the words even as I say them.

"You kept making excuses, pushing it off. What was I supposed to do?"

"I don't know; maybe let me handle it in my own way." I shake my head.

"I'm sorry." He reaches for me, but I shove his hand away.

"Don't do you dare fucking touch me," I grind out. "I told you I was doing it today. You had no right to take this into your own hands. This wasn't your call."

"Like hell it wasn't," he roars, his temper flaring for the first time. "Are you really that fucking blind that you can't see what you being with him is doing to me?"

"You did this to yourself. I was his before I was yours," I counter.

"You're mine. You've always been mine. You will always be mine. End of," he says, snagging my wrist in his hand. "You can be pissed and scream at me all you want, but at the end of the day I did you a favor whether you admit it now or not." He pulls me flush against his body. "You chose me. He needed to know that." He grips both of my shoulders in his hands, forcing me to meet his gaze.

"I fucking love you. I've never said that to anyone before. I'm so in love with you. I'm done with the barriers and obstacles. I just want you." His face is so close to mine I can feel the warmth of his breath as he speaks.

"Loving someone isn't forcing your way into their life and making their decisions for them. I'm sorry, Gavin, but I don't believe you love me because I don't think you know what love actually is." I push away from his hold, stumbling backward a couple of feet.

"Because you're such a fucking expert?" e bites. "Isn't loving someone trusting in them? You didn't trust me enough to tell me about your parents. You didn't trust me enough to tell Bryan the truth. And you don't trust me enough now. You don't trust that I love you because it's easier for you to push people away then to fucking let them see the real you."

"You're right, Gavin, I don't trust you. And clearly for good reason. I can't do this anymore. I'm sorry." Tears flood my vision as I push past him and take off toward my dorm.

My heart rips further and further apart with each step I take. By the time I reach my room, I feel like it's shredded into a million different pieces and the pain is beyond anything I have ever felt before.

I collapse onto my knees and succumb to the grief.

I let it take me under and swallow me whole.

Chapter Twenty-two

<u>Harlee</u>

"Why don't you come out with me and Decklan?" Kimber says, sitting on the side of my bed. "It will do you good to get out of this room."

"I don't want to go anywhere," I insist, refusing to look up from my laptop to meet her gaze.

"Harlee, it's been over a week. You can't just hide out in here for the rest of your life. What happened, happened. You have to pick yourself up and keep going," she says, resting her hand gently on my knee.

"I can't," I admit, sadness once again washing over me like a sudden wave smacking me in the face.

The first two days were filled with anger.

The next two with guilt.

Then came the regret. That was the worst.

I don't know how much more of this I can take.

Going to Gavin now seems like a lost cause. I don't feel like there's any coming back from the things I said or the way I treated him. I still don't agree with the way he handled things. But eventually, I came to understand. It was Angel and almost an entire bottle of tequila that made me see the light. And once it happened, it was like seeing myself through Gavin's eyes for the very first time.

To be honest, I didn't like what I saw.

"I don't want to leave you like this." Her voice is riddled with concern.

"I'll be fine. I promise. I just need some more time. I'm not ready to face a world without him yet," I admit, the statement causing the emotion to clog in my throat.

"He's still here ya know? You could call him."

"No, I can't. You didn't see his face. You didn't hear the awful things I said to him. There's no coming back."

"You don't know that unless you try," she insists.

"I'm not you, Kimber," I say, pushing the computer from my lap before pulling my knees to my chest. "I can't have endless amounts of faith and believe that everything will be okay because that's not always the case. I'm so happy things worked out for you and Decklan, but that doesn't mean that everyone gets a happy ending. Life doesn't work that way."

"I know that." She doesn't seem even the least bit offended by my rant. "I know things don't always turn out the way we want. But I also know that if you're not willing to fight for what you want, you'll live your life ruled by regret. Do you really want that?"

"What I want is Gavin."

"Then go to him. I don't think you grasp just how much that man cares about you. Decklan said he's never seen Gavin so torn up before. He drinks all day. He barely leaves his condo and that's only to go to the bar to get drunk. Paxton has been so worried about him he refuses to leave his side. His heart is broken, Harlee. Just like yours. You're both just too damn stubborn to get over yourselves and make the first move." Her tone turns almost aggravated.

"So you both made mistakes," she continues. "Big deal. What couple doesn't go through ups and downs. You need to get over yourself and at least call him, if not for you than for him."

"Why? He's made no attempt to contact me," I snip. "Why should I reach out to him?"

"Because someone has to make the first move," she replies simply.

"Well, it's not going to be me. I'm the one that came back running the last time, and I won't be the one to do it again. If he loves me as much as you say, then he will do something about it." I feel like a spoiled child, but I just can't help myself.

"Do you even hear yourself?" Kimber immediately calls me out on my behavior. "You two were made for each other."

She pushes into a stand, crossing toward the closet. Within moments she reappears with a pair of dark, low rise jeans and a three-quarter sleeve black top, tossing them into my lap.

"Get dressed," she orders. "Now," she tacks on, narrowing her eyes on my face, daring me to challenge her.

"I hate you," I huff, sliding from my bed.

I know there's no way she's going to leave if I don't agree to go with her and as much as I love her, I really don't feel like listening to her lecture me the entire night.

"You love me," she retorts, pulling a small smile from me.

"Fine, I love you." I spin toward the bathroom. "But right now I hate you a little, too," I call over my shoulder before disappearing inside.

****

"What the hell are we doing here?" I try to swallow down my panic, gripping the seatbelt running across my chest as Kimber pulls into the lot behind *Deviants*.

I knew as soon as she got onto the freeway that we were heading to Portland, but I just assumed we were meeting Decklan somewhere. I never dreamed in a million years she would bring me here.

"Relax." She puts her new car in park and kills the engine, turning her gaze to me. "He's not here."

"I don't care. Why would you bring me here?" I try to keep my anger in check, but I feel it seeping out of every word I speak.

"Because I thought maybe you would like to have a drink and unwind with friends. Considering this is the only place where you can actually drink..." She lets her statement hang there.

"You're unbelievable," I say in disbelief. "This was a setup all along." I shake my head, unable to believe that Kimber would force me into a situation I don't want to be in.

What is it with the people in my life forcing me to do things I don't want to do?

Maybe I should take this as a sign. Maybe I really am that blind. So much so that the people around me feel it's their duty to intervene. I shake away the idea, not willing to accept it.

"It's not a setup," she insists. "Gavin is at his condo. Charlie is there visiting him. She's promised to keep him put for the evening."

"Why would she do that?"

"Because Decklan asked her to. For me," she answers simply, pushing open the driver's side door. "Now are you just going to sit there or are you going to come have a drink with me? You know I'm gonna need a dance partner." She leans down, giving me a pretty please smile through the open car door.

"Who's the D.J.?" I ask, arms crossed firmly over my chest.

"Jam." She smirks, knowing she's got me.

Jam is the best D.J. at *Deviants* and always plays the best music to dance to when you're drunk and just need to shake some shit off.

"Fine," I grunt, shoving open the door. "But so help me, Kimber, if Gavin shows up here tonight I'll never forgive you," I warn, slamming the door shut behind me the moment I'm out of the way.

"If he shows up here, I'll throw him out myself." She gives me a wide grin, her eyes turning mischievous.

Honestly, I actually believe she would do it. The thought brings a smile to my face and even though I'm walking toward a place I never thought I'd enter again, I feel lighter than I have in days.

Kimber, like Angel, seems to know exactly what I need well before I even do. I really am so blessed to have them in my life. I honestly don't know how I would have survived this past week without them. They and Joy are the only reasons I haven't sunk into the dark hole I've been tempted to disappear inside of since the moment I walked away and left Gavin standing there in the courtyard what feels like weeks ago.

The usual Friday night line outside of *Deviants* is longer than usual, wrapping around the entire front of the building before disappearing around the corner. The bouncer simply nods when we approach, allowing us to slip behind him without a second glance.

The moment we step inside the music engulfs us, the heavy beat of a remix pop song thumping through the crowded space. Kimber grabs my hand and drags me through the sea of people toward the bar, stopping at the very edge of the counter.

"What do you want to drink?" She leans forward so I can hear her over the music.

"I don't care." I shrug. "Just make it

hard."

"That's what she said." She snickers, pulling an eye roll from me.

She knows how much I hate that statement. It was funny five years ago. Now it's just overused and honestly a bit annoying. I think that's exactly why she chose to say it in the first place.

She turns her attention back to the bar just seconds before Decklan appears in front of her. She immediately leans over the bar and lays a deep kiss to his mouth, not the least bit concerned about the group of women just to our right who are clearly watching the entire exchange between them, staring daggers into the side of Kimber's face.

The whole interaction makes my stomach twinge and for a moment I understand how the women next to us feel. Not because I want to be kissing Decklan—which they so clearly do, but because it makes me miss how it felt when I kissed Gavin that way.

Decklan throws me a half smile and nods just seconds after Kimber pulls back, grabbing my hand to pull me up to the bar.

"She needs something strong," Kimber yells over the roar of the music.

"I got just the thing." His smile widens.

Kimber turns back to me as Decklan busies himself making our drinks.

"Why is he bartending?" I question, knowing it's not something he does often.

Where Gavin loves working behind the bar, Decklan usually only does it if he absolutely has to, preferring to spend his time on the other side of the bar.

"Matt called off and since I asked that he keep a certain someone away, he had to fill in." She shakes her head when she sees the immediate guilt that creeps across my face. "Don't." She rests her hand on my forearm. "He was happy to do it."

"I bet he'd be much happier spending time with you," I interject, feeling like a bit of a burden.

"He's just as happy doing things that make me happy. You being here makes me happy." She winks, turning her attention back to the bar as Decklan reappears holding two very large, orange drinks garnished with fresh fruit.

"Don't let the looks deceive you." He catches my confused stare. "They'll knock you right on your ass," he promises, turning his attention to Kimber. "Only one for you," he adds, pulling a laugh from her.

"Yes, sir." She winks, sticking her tongue out at him. "He clearly knows that I am a total light weight." She turns toward me just as she takes a drink from her straw, her eyes immediately going wide. "Holy shit." She looks at the drink like she's trying to somehow figure out what's in it.

I mirror her actions, pulling a long draw from my straw. The fruity concoction hits my tongue, the overwhelming taste of orange and pineapple dancing across my taste buds. I have no idea why Kimber reacted the way she did. That is until I swallow and a sudden fire engulfs my throat.

"What the hell?" I look up wide-eyed at Kimber.

"I know, right," she laughs, taking another drink.

Sliding into the two empty stools in front of us, it's not long before the alcohol has worked its way into my blood stream and everything starts to feel a little less heavy. Kimber rambles on about her and Decklan's wedding for a good thirty minutes, telling me every detail about how they plan to elope this summer. It's her subtle way of telling me she's moving out at the end of the spring term but after two drinks I barely even process the news.

Decklan's right, these drinks are no joke. I make a mental note to ask him what's in them the next time he comes over, though it's likely I'll forget by then.

I'm not really sure how much time passes before I sense someone beside me. I turn to see Paxton settled into the stool next to me, his handsome face pulled into a tight scowl.

"You look so happy right now," I joke, my words bordering on a slur.

Shit, I think I'm a little drunk.

"Yeah, well." He shrugs, nodding toward Val, who within seconds has a beer sitting on the bar in front of him.

"Wanna talk about it?" I ask, not sure I really want to know.

"Nope." He raises the beer bottle to his lips and drains half the bottle in one drink.

"That bad huh?" I kick my leg over Kimber's stool when a college-aged man tries to sit down. "Taken." I smile, immediately wondering what is taking Kimber so long in the bathroom. I feel like she's been gone forever.

"You have no idea." He sighs, pulling my attention back to him.

"Girl trouble?" I question.

"Something like that."

"Well, you've come to the right place. I'm having major girl trouble." It takes me a moment to realize what I just said, giggling the instant it dawns on me. "I mean boy trouble," I correct. "I like boys, not girls. I mean, I like dick. Oh my god. I just said that out loud, didn't I?" I ramble, watching as Paxton's lips turn up in an amused smile.

"You're cute." He drinks the remainder

of his beer in one more long gulp, sliding the empty bottle across the bar. "I can see why Gavin is so taken with you," he adds, nodding once again when Val slides another beer across the bar to him.

"Yeah, not so much anymore." I sigh, leaning forward to take a sip out of my own drink.

"Maybe someone should tell him that." He chuckles, lifting the beer bottle to his lips. "From where I'm sitting, he's still very much taken with you."

"Yeah well, from where I'm sitting, I'm pretty sure he hates my guts. Love sucks," I grind out, once again catching the slur in my voice. "Where the hell is Kimber?" I change course without warning.

"I saw her and Decklan go upstairs on my way in," He answers without looking in my direction.

"Fucking whore," I blurt, covering my mouth when once again the words meant for my mind flow out.

Paxton makes a choking noise as he struggles to swallow his beer before bursting out in laughter. "You have no fucking filter. You realize this right?"

"Me?" I question. "That's completely untrue. Didn't you hear, I'm the coward who hides behind her own excuses."

"Well, that's okay because I'm the

asshole who dicks over his friend and completely fucks everything up every chance he gets." I can tell by his reaction that he regrets his statement the moment he makes it.

I suspect his current mood has something to do with Charlie, but I keep that assumption to myself. It's clear it's not something anyone knows about, if there's anything going on at all. Maybe I'm just seeing things that aren't there. It certainly wouldn't be the first time.

"We should start a club," I offer, holding my drink up.

"And what should we call said club?" He turns toward me, a small smirk on his face.

"How about *The Fuck Love Club*?" I suggest.

"Fuck love," he agrees, clinking his beer bottle against my glass before we both drink.

There's a smile on my lips the moment I resurface from the bottom of my glass. While Paxton and I have said nothing at all, we've also said so much. For the first time since ending things with Gavin, I feel a little less alone in this world.

That is until I register Paxton's expression, his eyes focused on something across the room. I follow his line of sight, all the air rushing from my body when I see Gavin standing at the other end of the bar, his eyes locked firmly on my face.

And he doesn't look happy to see me...

Chapter Twenty-three

Gavin

I can't take my eyes off of her. She seems fine. Happy even. How the fuck can she just sit there, laughing and drinking with one of *my* best friends, in *my* fucking bar, like everything is just fucking peachy?

Anger flares in my chest, my gaze darting toward Paxton who catches sight of me instantly, the smile falling from his face.

Yeah, you better quit smiling at my girl, you mother fucker.

My girl?

Too bad she's not my fucking girl anymore.

I watch in slow motion as Harlee looks

toward Paxton and then follows his gaze, her eyes finding mine within seconds. I watch her face fall in shock followed by the deep flush that fills her cheeks, evident even in the dim bar lighting.

She makes no attempt to move or even really react for that matter. She just sits there, staring at me like she's seeing a ghost.

I break eye contact when the door beside me opens, Decklan and Kimber suddenly appearing just feet from where I'm standing. I can see the panic that immediately floods Kimber's pretty face and the apology written across Decklan's when he meets my gaze.

Now I know why Charlie tried so damn hard to keep my ass at home. She knew Harlee was here. Every single one of these fuckers knew she was here and what's worse? They purposely kept her from me.

The sting of their betrayal is real, but it barely registers on my already pain-riddled heart. I don't think anything can hurt me the way Harlee did. And as such, everything else seems like a tiny blip in comparison.

I look back at Harlee to find her eyes are still locked in my direction.

"Gavin." Decklan lays a hand on my shoulder, pulling my attention back to him.

"Don't." I shake his hand off my shoulder. "When you pissed away what you had with Kimber, who was there to help you get her back? Who hand delivered her to you? I did. This is how you repay me? You bring Harlee here and then get my little sister to play babysitter to make sure I don't find out?"

"This is my fault," Kimber immediately interrupts. "I asked him to do it," she admits apologetically. "I just wanted to get her out of her room."

"And you couldn't have done that somewhere else?" I bite, knowing the moment it leaves my mouth that I'm treading on very thin ice. The way Decklan steps in front of Kimber to shield her from me is all the indication I need.

"Careful," he warns.

"Fuck you, Deck," I spit, anger seething through me. "Good to see when I need a true friend I have none."

"That's bullshit and you know it. We're brothers man." He clasps his hand on my shoulder again, this time tightening his grip enough that I can't easily shake him off. "I wanted to respect what Kimber was trying to do for her friend without rubbing her in your face. This isn't some big conspiracy against you. I was trying to spare you." He tightens his hand on my shoulder, forcing me to meet his gaze.

"You should have told me." I grind out.

"I'm sorry." His apology is genuine, that much I can tell. But it does nothing to slow the flames that have burst to life in my chest.

I nod, letting him know we're good before turning my gaze back to the end of the bar, my heart dropping into my stomach when I realize she's no longer there. I look to Paxton who shrugs apologetically and gestures toward the door.

I immediately set off in that direction, ignoring the sound of Kimber calling my name behind me. I may have been able to kid myself into believing that I could live without Harlee, but after seeing her just moments ago, I realize how very wrong I was.

Not only can I not live without her, but I don't fucking want to.

I look left and then right, scanning the sidewalk the moment I step outside. Turning left when I don't see her anywhere. I quickly round the building, stopping dead in my tracks when I spot Harlee leaning against the wall, her gaze turned downward.

"I should never have pushed you away," she says so quietly I don't know if she's talking to herself or if she's completely aware that I'm standing just feet from her.

"I messed things up so bad," she chokes out, emotion clear in her voice.

If I didn't know any better I'd say she's talking to the wind, having still made no attempt to look my way.

"I'm so sorry." When she finally looks

up, her eyes are glassed over in tears, her expression pained. "I'm so, so sorry, Gavin." Her words slur slightly, giving away her clear intoxication.

"You're drunk." It's a statement, not a question, my voice coming out a bit harsher than I really intend for it to.

"Maybe a little," she admits. "But if I wasn't I wouldn't have stopped here. I would have run away, left, too ashamed and embarrassed to face you after the way I treated you."

"You have nothing to be ashamed of." I take a hesitant step forward. "It's me that should be ashamed. I was completely out of line."

"You were right." She cuts me off, her gaze halting my movements.

"No, I wasn't." I shake my head.

"You made me feel things I didn't know I could feel. It scared the shit out of me," she admits. "I didn't know how to handle those feelings. So I hid. I hid behind Bryan. I hid behind my fear. Even when I knew you were what I wanted, I couldn't make myself act on it. I couldn't take that final step, afraid that once I did, everything would fall apart. I was convinced you were in it for the chase, for the game. That once you had me, I mean really had me, you would no longer want me."

"You couldn't have been more wrong," I

cut in, taking another step toward her, closing the distance between us to just a couple feet.

"I should have trusted you. I should have trusted us." She wipes at a stray tear that escapes her eye.

"How I feel about you, it scared me too, Harlee. It fucking terrified me. It still does," I admit. I should have given you the time you needed to work through your hesitation instead of forcing you into something you weren't ready for," I add.

"But I was ready. I wanted to be with you from the moment I first saw you. I knew you were it. I think that's what scared me more than anything; how quickly I fell for you." She lets out a slow breath. "I was ready. I still am. But now it's too late."

"Who said it's too late?" I can't help the smile that pulls at the corner of my mouth.

"You did," she continues when she sees the confusion that crosses my face. "You left. You didn't fight for me. You didn't call me. You made no attempt to contact me at all. If that doesn't tell me you're done, I don't know what would." She swipes at another tear.

"I'm not done. Far from it." I close the distance between us, taking her face in my hands. "I was trying to respect your wishes, something I should have done from the very beginning. I thought I was doing the right thing by leaving you alone. Every single fucking day without you has been worse than the last. It gutted me to leave you that day. It fucking killed me to stay away from you. I love you, Harlee. So fucking much it hurts," I breathe, pressing my mouth firmly to hers.

Her body relaxes against me as she melts into the kiss. Only seconds pass before her fingers find their normal spot, tangling in the back of my hair as she tightens her grip on me.

It feels so good to have her body pressed against mine again. To feel her bottom lip quiver as I slide my tongue into her mouth. To hear her soft moans as I kiss her harder, deeper, wanting to make sure she never has the power to walk away from me ever again.

"Say you're mine," I speak against her lips. "I need you to say it. I need you to mean it this time. I need you to be mine."

"I was always yours." Her response is instant.

A wide smile spreads across her beautiful face as her fingers tighten their grip on my hair, pulling my lips back down to hers.

Chapter Twenty-four

Harlee

Words simply cannot describe the way it feels to be back in Gavin's arms. To see him drop all his walls and let me see his true vulnerability. I don't think I realized just how much I hurt him by pushing him away. Something I promise myself right here and now to never do again.

"I love you," he breathes against my lips, resting his forehead against mine. "Don't fucking break my heart again. I don't think it could take it." He pulls back, his eyes locked firmly on mine.

"That goes for you, too." I cup his cheek and lose myself in the depths of his blue eyes.

"We should probably head back inside," I add on. "I'm sure they are wondering where we disappeared to." I refer to Kimber, Decklan, and Paxton who are still inside the bar.

"I could care less." He drops a light kiss to my lips.

"You mean you couldn't care less?" I let out a small laugh. "Saying you could care less means you *could* actually care less."

"Yeah, that's what I said," he laughs, the sound the most amazing thing I've ever heard.

"So you do care or you don't?" I can't quite keep up with what he's trying to say.

"I don't."

"So then you couldn't care less."

"That's what I said," he teases.

"Okay." I shake my head, knowing at this point he's purposely just trying to confuse me for his own amusement.

Glad to see some things never change.

"I'm more concerned about getting home and kicking Charlie's devious ass to the curb so I can show my girlfriend just how fucking much I love her for the rest of the night." He gives me a wicked smile, his eyes boring into mine.

"Your girlfriend huh?" I joke. "She must be an incredible woman to have earned the title of *your* girlfriend."

"Oh, you have no idea. Not only is she

the most beautiful creature I've ever laid eyes on, she also sucks a mean cock." He busts out laughing when my mouth drops open in shock.

"I cannot believe you just said that." I shake my head on a laugh. "Wait. Yes, I can." I laugh harder.

"So is that a yes?" he asks, falling serious.

"Did you ask me a question?" I stare up at him in confusion.

"Seriously?" He hits me with a fake look of annoyance. "Stop playing fucking games with me, Harlee," he growls, nipping at my bottom lip.

"I didn't realize I was," I answer truthfully.

"Will you be my fucking girlfriend or not?" He pulls back so he can study my reaction, but it's his that I can't seem to get past.

He seems...nervous.

The thought seems odd to me and yet so completely endearing at the same time. It's like we're suddenly teenagers again and he's asking me to prom, fearful that I might say no.

"That's not even a question," I interject playfully.

"Yes, it fucking is. Stop playing with me, woman," he warns, grinding himself into my core causing my entire body to zing to life.

"Now answer the question." His voice drops low as his lips hover just inches from mine.

"It's not a question because you already know the answer. I belong to you, Gavin Porter. Call me whatever you want. I'm yours."

"A simple yes or no please." He gently sucks my bottom lip into his mouth, pulling a light moan from my throat.

I don't know why he needs to hear me say it. I don't know why labeling me as his girlfriend is so important to him. But I do know that there's nothing more I want to be. I meant it when I said he owned me. He has always owned me. I'm just done fighting against it now.

"Yes," I purr against his mouth, feeling his smile spread against my lips.

"Yes," he responds, more a victory statement than him repeating my words.

A soft laugh escapes my mouth as he presses into me and kisses me once more, this time with so much intensity I swear I can feel the effects of him everywhere. From the tips of my fingers to the very ends of each toe, there is not one part of my body that doesn't feel his presence.

"Now." He pulls back just far enough to meet my gaze. "How about we get out of here so we can *really* make up?" He raises his eyebrows up and down suggestively.

"Again, not even a question." I smile,

screaming in surprise when he bends down and throws me over his shoulder with next to no effort. "Gavin!" I protest, squirming in his grasp.

"I love it when you scream my name." I can feel his body vibrate beneath me as laughter rolls through him.

"Well you know, there are much more effective ways to achieve that," I interject.

"Oh, believe me, I know. The night is still young." There is so much promise in his voice, my stomach clenches tightly in anticipation.

He crosses the parking lot like I weigh nothing. Tossing me into the truck like a twenty-pound sack of potatoes rather than an actual person. He gives me an earth-bending smile the moment he slides in next to me, pulling me to the center of the seat so I'm sitting directly next to him.

"God. My boyfriend is so needy," I whine playfully.

"You're damn right I am. You better fucking get used to it, too. Cause I'm not letting you get rid of me anytime soon." His smile only spreads as he stares back at me, his eyes locked firmly on mine.

****

As I lay next to a sleeping Gavin,

watching his chest rise and fall with each deep breath he takes, I can't help but think about all the moments that led us here, to this time and place. The lows and highs, the tears and laughter. It seems like so long ago I was just a girl and he was just another guy.

I don't know when this happened. When we went from hooking up, to falling in love, to falling apart, to finding ourselves forever lost in each other.

I don't know when the scared, hesitant girl vanished and this new confident, determined woman took her place. Was it days ago when I thought I had lost Gavin forever or was it merely hours ago as I sat at the bar wishing he was the one sitting next to me?

I don't know when I found myself exactly or if I can even take credit for it all.

Gavin did all the work.

All I had to do was close my eyes and hang on for dear life, praying like hell that when I opened them again I would find myself exactly where I am. In the arms of a man who not only pushed me to my very limits but who also showed me what it meant to love.

The real kind of love. The crazy, stupid, obsessive kind of love. The kind of love that swallows you up and refuses to never let you go.

Gavin Porter didn't just consume me, he

owned me from that very first night.

I told him I was his. I've never spoken a truer statement.

I have always been his...

And now, he is mine...

The End

Crazy Stupid Obsession Playlist

A special thank you to these amazing musicians for sharing their talent with the world.

Addicted- Kelly Clarkson
All in my Head- Tori Kelly
Misery- Gwen Stefani
Close- Nick Jonas
Beating Me Up- Rachel Platten
All the Same- Sick Puppies
This Close- Flyleaf
Not Even Human- Angel Taylor
Vulnerable- Secondhand Serenade
Need the Sun to Break- James Bay
H.O.L.Y.- Florida Georgia Line
Heavy In Your Arms- Florence and the Machine
Heart Go Bang- Blue October
Fire Away- Chris Stapleton

Connect with
Melissa Toppen

www.mtoppen.com
www.facebook.com/mtoppenauthor
www.facebook.com/melissatoppen
www.goodreads.com/mtoppen
www.twitter.com/mtoppenauthor
www.tsu.co/mtoppenauthor
www.instagram.com/melissa_toppen
www.pinterest.com/mtoppenauthor

0854

38510082R00182

Made in the USA
San Bernardino, CA
07 September 2016